Reikan
The most haunted locations in Japan
Vol. 1

Tara A. Devlin

Visit the author's website at www.taraadevlin.com or www.kowabana.net

© 2018 Tara A. Devlin

All rights reserved. No portion of this book may be reproduced in any form without permission from the publisher, except as permitted by U.S. copyright law.

DEDICATION

To everyone who has joined me on this crazy journey, and to Japan for providing so many great stories over the years.

CONTENTS

Introduction

1 Hokkaido 1

2 Tohoku 17

3 Kanto 47

4 Chubu 111

5 Kansai 141

6 Chugoku 163

7 Shikoku 187

8 Kyushu 203

INTRODUCTION

"Ultimately, ghost hunting is not about the evidence (if it was, the search would have been abandoned long ago). Instead, it's about having fun with friends, telling stories, and the enjoyment of pretending they are searching the edge of the unknown. After all, everyone loves a good ghost story." *-Benjamin Radford, Live Science Contributor [http://www.livescience.com/26697-are-ghosts-real.html]*

I don't believe in ghosts.

Now that that's out of the way, let me take this opportunity to say that I *love* ghost stories. I have ever since I was a child, and it's difficult to explain why. Maybe it's the unknown. Maybe it's the fear factor. Maybe part of me wants to believe that there's something out there after death, and ghost stories are a way of fulfilling that.

For 10 years I lived in Matsue, the self-proclaimed "home of Japanese ghost stories." In 1890, Greek-Irish journalist Lafcadio Hearn moved to Matsue. He took up teaching and then met the woman who would later become his wife. Over the years Hearn lived in Japan, he compiled several ghost tales and, with the help of his wife, translated them into English for the first time. The stories then spread out into the world and became the West's first glimpse of what *kaidan*, or ghost stories, Japan had to offer.

I heard about all sorts of haunted locations—or ghost spots, as they're called in Japanese—while I was living in Matsue. I went on late night drives with my friends, like many of the people in this book do. We went ghost hunting, driving along lonely roads and looking for abandoned buildings or places with a story to tell. Because it is in those stories that you discover the truth of humanity. Who we are and what we're capable of. Every ghost spot has a story to tell, if you're willing to go digging for it. Perhaps someone was brutally murdered. Perhaps there was a tragic accident. Or perhaps there was really nothing at all, and over time people made up a story in remembrance of a place that once held special meaning for them.

In this book, you'll find tales of murder, suicide, and numerous real-life tragedies from locations from all over Japan. Hospitals, abandoned buildings, tunnels, waterfalls, mountains, caves; if it's haunted, it's here. You'll discover some of the most famous ghost stories that go along with each place, as well as general information on the location and what hauntings you can expect to find if you go there yourself.

Whether ghosts are real or not is up to you to decide for yourself. But their stories provide us with a real insight into the human condition, and at the end of the day, are just plain fun to read. Japan has long held close ties to the spirit world, and that plays a large part in many of these stories. The fact that someone can die and become attached to that place is a given for many and not questioned. Ghost hunting is almost a sport for some, and you can find countless blogs on the internet today that detail people's adventures into known ghost spots.

So step inside and take a terrifying trip around the world from the safety and comfort of your armchair. These ghost spots are nothing like what you've heard of in the West. Let's hunt some *yurei*.

HOKKAIDO

Jomon Tunnel

Location: Kanehana, Rubeshibe-cho, Kitami City, Hokkaido Prefecture, 091-0021

A man was on the night train travelling through Hokkaido. As it approached the Jomon Tunnel, he suddenly heard a whistle.

"Is there a deer on the tracks?" the man thought, but as the train went further into the tunnel, the whistle continued.

He got under the covers and tried to go to sleep, despite the noise, but then he sensed something passing by his cabin door. He nervously approached the door to look out the tiny window installed in it. Afraid of what he might see, the man worked up the courage to take a peek. He looked out into the hall and saw a black shadow slowly passing by.

It wasn't a person. It was in the shape of a person, sure, but it wasn't one. He could see the wall on the other side of it. It was semi-transparent, like a ghost. A few moments later it disappeared.

He looked at the ground and saw wet footprints where the shadow had just been. Then he saw the conductor walking down the hall. He bent down to wipe the wet footprints away.

"Sir, did you just see that?" the conductor stood up and asked. The man looked at the tissue in his hand. It was stained red with blood…

Jomon Tunnel is part of the JR Hokkaido Line in Kitami, Hokkaido. The tunnel is situated on the

Sekihoku Main Line between Ikutahara and Nishi-Rubeshibe stations and cuts through the Jomon Ridge. Construction began in 1912 and was completed in 1914. At 347 metres above sea level and running 507 metres in length, the tunnel runs through a difficult section of the Jomon Ridge in the middle of nowhere. The tunnel is often called the place with the cruellest history in all of Japan. But how did it manage to get that reputation, and why is it considered one of the most well-known haunted locations in Japan today?

Construction on the tunnel began in 1912 with the use of *tako* labourers. Tako labourers first came into existence on the island of Hokkaido in 1887 as prison labourers. Vast areas of Hokkaido were, at that point, still untouched by the modernity of civilisation, and these men were forced into building roads and railways to connect the far-flung cities and villages. By 1894, however, the Meiji government declared that the prisoners being forced into such difficult work in the horrendously cold Hokkaido weather was inhumane, and the practice was stopped.

Officially, anyway.

Work had to continue, so labourers were instead recruited from the main island of Honshu under the guise of legitimate work. The workers were holed up in *tako* rooms and stripped of their basic human rights. These tako rooms were tight living quarters that were easily and quickly built near construction sites. They were small wooden bungalows usually made with pine logs and thatched roofing that fit around 70 men. To stop men from escaping during the night, there was a single sliding door with a bell to alert camp leaders when someone was trying to enter or exit the room. The door was also able to be locked from the outside. With only tiny slits for windows, the rooms received almost no light and had very little ventilation.

The men were watched over by an *oyakata*, a master, who had several men working below him; the manager, reception, head labourer, and supervisor. The tako labourers were themselves split up into three groups; the upper-class dining, the middle-class dining, and the lower-class dining. The men who worked beneath the oyakata were upper-class and were able to eat in a separate room come meal time. The majority of tako labourers made up the lower-class and were forced to stand when having meals. Those who worked particularly well, however, were rewarded by being moved up to the middle-class, where they were allowed a bench to sit on during meals. In order to control these men, the labourers often faced false imprisonment, assault, exploitation and oppression. They weren't prisoners, technically, but they were treated like them, regardless.

By now you probably have some idea of the horrible conditions the tako labourers were forced to live under when they were working. The men were forced to work 15-hour days without break. On top of the physically demanding work and incredibly cold Hokkaido weather, the men working on the Jomon Tunnel were only given meagre meals; rice twice a day with a side of miso soup. By the time the tunnel was completed, over 100 labourers had died. Thanks to the hard labour and malnutrition, men started to collapse one after the other due to beriberi, a chronic form of thiamine deficiency. And yet they were not given medical care; the men instead faced corporal punishment and their bodies were buried in a mass grave in the forest close to the tunnel. There are legends that locals who stumbled upon the area while gathering edible plants collected their bones for burial.

Men who tried to escape also faced harsh punishments. Once they were caught, the men were brutally assaulted and, in the worst cases, tied naked to trees and lynched. If they died during such punishments, they were tossed in a pile with the rest of the dead bodies.

After the tunnel opened, it was plagued with troubles. One story goes that an engineer was driving his steam train inside Jomon Tunnel one evening, not long after construction had finished, when he saw a man standing before him, blood pouring from his head. The engineer quickly stopped the train and ran out to check, but when he got there, the man was gone.

He returned to the train and started it once more, but he again saw the man standing before him with blood pouring from his head. He stopped the train again, but the man's dreadful expression was burned into his eyes. He closed his eyes and waited for the train to stop, but another train was approaching from behind. He got out and informed the driver of the other train what was going on. The driver agreed to switch places with him, and the engineer followed in the other train from behind.

But it wasn't just inside the tunnel. Passengers claimed they could hear moaning that sounded like someone was suffocating close to the tunnel, and a station attendant who worked at Jomon Station went mad and fell ill to a mysterious disease. It didn't just affect those nearby either. The mysterious happenings near the tunnel even extended to family members. Yet another station attendant's wife threw herself in front of a train inside the tunnel and killed herself.

People blamed these incidents on the spirits of the dead, and in 1959, a Kanwa Jizo statue was erected about one kilometre from the tunnel. This was an area where the skeletons of roughly 50 railway workers and their family members were discovered. But in 1968, the Tokachi Earthquake hit with a magnitude of 7.9 on the Richter scale. The walls of the Jomon Tunnel were damaged, and work started once more to repair them in 1970. It was at this time that the skeletons of over 100 workers from the original tunnel were discovered near the entrance and in the woods nearby. The bones were broken and showed evidence of violence and mistreatment. It was here, over 50 years later, that people finally discovered what horrible conditions the original labourers were forced to work in.

In September of the same year, Jomon Station (currently Jomon Signal Station) was undergoing expansions when a skull was found in the gravel roughly 60 centimetres from the brick wall near the exit. There had long been rumours that *hitobashira* were used in the construction of Jomon Tunnel. Hitobashira, literally 'human pillars,' were people sacrificed in prayer to the gods to avoid disaster. They were either buried inside the building like a pillar, buried in the earth, or submerged in nearby water. They were, of course, alive during this whole process. The sacrifice was only worthy if the hitobashira was alive when being buried.

The discovery of a skull by the station wall appeared to confirm this practice to be true, and one station attendant claimed that "there's a good chance there are more of them around here." He also claimed that everyone who worked there knew the wall had a hitobashira inside. And indeed, more skeletons were found standing up inside the walls of Jomon Tunnel during reconstruction. The state of the skeletons and the position they were found in led people to believe that the labourers hadn't been buried in the walls after death, but rather forced in while they were still alive. They were later moved to the nearby Rubeshibe public cemetery for reburial.

In 1980, a monument was erected in Rubeshibe City looking down over the Sekihoku Main Line near Kanehana Station. This monument was in commemoration of all the victims who died during the construction of Jomon Tunnel, but it doesn't appear to have appeased the dead. On the contrary, hauntings and strange occurrences reportedly continue in the area to this day.

Monami Park

Location: 1 Chome, Kawazoe 10 Jo, Minami Ward, Sapporo, Hokkaido Prefecture, 005-0810

As the Meiji Era was coming to an end, there was a man named Wakatsuki Tamekichi who ran a store in Susukino, Sapporo, selling kimono fabrics. In order to gather more stock for his store, he took a trip all the way to Tokyo, half a country away. While there, he remembered the Yoshiwara red-light district and went over for a visit. There, he procured himself a courtesan and took her back to Sapporo with him.

But the courtesan was in love with a man in Tokyo and did not wish to be in Sapporo any longer. After three months of confinement, she told Tamekichi her wish to leave.

Tamekichi responded by building a tower and locking the courtesan inside, and each day inside was like a living hell for the young woman. She cried and screamed, but not even the servants could hear her.

One night, however, the courtesan finally escaped the tower. She ran all the way to the Toyohira River, several kilometres away, and stood upon a cliff facing the deep, dark abyss below. With no options left, she jumped.

Her body was later found holding her courtesan's umbrella and wearing her tall wooden clogs. Thereafter, the cliff the courtesan threw herself from came to be known as the Courtesan's Abyss…

In 1949, Monami Park was established. The waters of the Toyohira River used to be much higher than they are now, but you can still visit the very same cliff the courtesan was said to have jumped from inside the park. Not only that, but rumours persist that over 100 years later, the courtesan's spirit continues to linger in the area, unable to move on because of the terrible circumstances leading up to her death. People claim to feel themselves being tugged to the cliff's edge when walking by, or they are suddenly overcome with the desire to jump over the edge themselves.

But the courtesan isn't the only spirit that lingers in the area.

In the early 2000s, a police officer from the Hokkaido Prefectural Police Department was wrapped up in a scandal involving drugs, corruption, and illegal firing of a weapon. His body was found hanging in the male toilets not too far from the Courtesan's Abyss.

In a separate incident, a police officer at the end of his shift was returning to the main station when he instead dropped by the *koban*, or police box, at Monami Park instead. There, he shot himself. The reason why remains unknown. What could drive two different police officers, at different times, to kill themselves in the same area? The curse of the courtesan? Or simply an unlucky coincidence?

Other rumours exist about the park as well. People claim to hear the voice of a crying baby coming from the public toilets where the police officer killed himself, even though no-one is inside. Bodies are often found drowned in the Toyohira

River, particularly in the area known as the Courtesan's Abyss; the deepest and most dangerous part. Other ghosts supposedly appear in the area as well, perhaps drawn to the spiritual energy first created when the courtesan threw herself to her death all those years ago. Japanese ghosts love water and suicides. Combine the two and you have yourself a popular ghost spot.

Yuubetsu Coal Mine

Location: Road 667, Yuubetsu 22 Sen, Akan-cho, Kushiro City, Hokkaido Prefecture, 085-0000

It was October. The nights were starting to get longer, and the weather colder. A young man from Obihiro, in Hokkaido, decided to head towards the abandoned Yuubetsu Coal Mine with three of his friends for a little test of courage. Who would prove to be the manliest of them all? They were about to find out.

They piled into the car and drank merrily on the way. By the time they reached the mine late that night, the men were well and truly drunk.

Of course, the group of young friends were entirely alone, not another soul in sight. Laughing and telling jokes, they approached the abandoned mining town in high spirits. Their goal was the infamous hospital, said to be the most dangerous spot of all.

They shone their torches as they stepped inside the building. It was covered in graffiti, a sign of all who had ventured there before them. The pitch black building was creepy. So creepy that the young man felt himself sober up rather quickly.

They reached a terrace inside the building when suddenly they heard a high-pitched scream. It was a woman's scream. The group consisted of four men, and they didn't sense anyone else inside the building when they entered. The young man panicked and fled, his friends hot on his heels.

Once they were safely outside, the young man turned and shone his torch on the entrance. He could hear the sound of countless footsteps running around inside, but he couldn't see anyone in the light of his torch. The group ran back to their car as fast as their feet would carry them, unable to withstand it any longer.

As soon as they got in, the young man's phone rang. 'Who could that be?' he wondered and took the phone out of his pocket. The caller said "Unknown number." He looked up to the corner of the screen. The phone was out of range.

It continued to ring.

His friends pleaded with the young man to get the hell out of there. He pressed 'answer' on his phone and put the receiver to his ear. What sounded like a strong wind was blowing on the other end, but somewhere, deep in the distance, he could hear voices talking.

Then, suddenly, he heard that shriek again. The one from the hospital. It was so loud that everyone in the car heard it. The young man hung up.

Everyone else's phones rang all at once. They took off in the car, back towards town. The phones continued to ring the entire way, and it wasn't until they reached civilisation that they all stopped at the same time.

The group never went back to the mining town again, but immediately after, the young man changed his phone for a new one. Just in case…

In 2007, the Ministry of Economy, Trade and Industry (METI) in Japan designated the Yuubetsu

Coal Mine in Hokkaido as a "Heritage of Industrial Modernisation." The mine and its nearby railroad opened on January 17, 1923, and by 1964, it was seeing record coal production that helped propel Japanese industry to new heights. A town was built around the prosperous mine with its own hospital, school, and even theatre. Over 10,000 people lived there at its height.

However, accident after accident gutted the mine, and in 1970 it was closed for good. These days, it sits abandoned deep in the mountains of Hokkaido, nature reclaiming what was once hers. But thanks to the METI designation, efforts are being undertaken to preserve this important piece of Japanese history.

As you might expect from its inclusion in this book, and the opening story, these days the Yuubetsu Coal Mine is also said to be haunted.

The once proud buildings that stood tall and strong by the coal mine, full of life and laughter, now stand empty and abandoned. Shells of their former selves. Now little more than a dumping ground for unwanted rubbish, the once clean walls are now marked with graffiti by local teenagers who use the site for their *kimodameshi*, or tests of courage, during the night.

It was a series of horrific accidents over the years that eventually brought the coal mine to an end.

    1933: Gas explosion (5 dead, several injured)
    1935: Gas explosion (95 dead)
    1955: Gas explosion (60 dead, 77 injured)
    1967: Cave-in (6 dead)

1968: Collapse (4 dead)
1969: Gas explosion (19 dead, 24 injured)

The mine saw 189 people die inside its walls over the 47 years it was in operation, and a memorial stone to those who lost their lives on the job can now be found in the forest outside. As the mine closed and people moved away, the city that had once thrived became a ghost town. Literally, according to some.

The hospital in particular is said to be the most haunted area in town, and consequently, the most dangerous. Merely stepping foot inside the building can result in sudden and inexplicable dizziness, migraines, and uncontrollable shivering. It doesn't matter how strong your *reikan*, or ability to sense the supernatural, is. The spiritual energy trapped inside the hospital is so strong, and so violent, that even ordinary folk who've never seen a ghost in their lives can be afflicted by it. The operating room and morgue are said to be the worst... if you can make it that far.

The hospital was completed only two years before the mine went out of operation. It was brand new. It wasn't built on the ruins of an old hospital, nor another building that might have transferred its angry spirits over. Some have questioned the validity of the hospital being the most violent of all buildings in the abandoned town, considering its lack of history. But it was in operation for two gas explosions, serving all who were killed and injured inside. Hospitals have been haunted for less.

Whether the hospital, the town, or even the mine

itself are actually haunted is up to each person to decide for him or herself. But thanks to the METI designation of Yuubetsu Coal Mine as a Heritage of Industrial Modernisation, at the very least, if any spirits do remain in the area today, they can rest well knowing their home will soon be well protected.

TOHOKU

Hakkoda Mountains

Location: Kansuizawa, Arakawa, Aomori City, Aomori Prefecture, 030-0111

A young man was on his way home with his date through the Hakkoda Mountains late one night. They were approaching the infamous bronze statue of Corporal Goto, one of the few survivors of a tragic accident that took the lives of hundreds of soldiers in the mountains over 100 years earlier.

His girlfriend suddenly felt a pain in her back, like something heavy was being pushed against it. Being where they were, she didn't want to say anything to worry her boyfriend, so she kept quiet. But the longer she stayed silent, the more the pain grew, until finally she couldn't take it anymore.

"My back… there's something wrong with my back…"

As she explained what was going on, her boyfriend muttered a prayer to Buddha and slapped her on the back, over and over. She joined him in prayer, hoping it would do something to ease her pain. But it wasn't until they were through the mountains where so many soldiers lost their lives and back in the safety of the city that the pain suddenly vanished…

The time was 6:55 a.m. on January 23, 1902. It was a bitterly cold winter morning in Aomori, the northernmost prefecture on the island of Honshu. Average January temperatures were below zero, and heavy snowfall was the norm. The Imperial Japanese Army's Fifth Infantry Regiment was stationed in Aomori City, the largest and most important city on the northern tip of Honshu. War with neighbouring Russia was looming on the horizon, and the Imperial Army was fearful of an attack sooner rather than later.

They decided they needed to secure a route inland through the Hakkoda Mountains just in case the Imperial Russian Navy destroyed roads and railways along the coast. If that came to be, it would make the Imperial Japanese Army's job of defending their home soil all the more difficult. The Russians would be able to invade and they would be unable to stop them. They couldn't let that happen.

The Fifth Infantry Regiment consisted of 3,000 men. Of those, 210 were chosen for the expedition. Few of these men had experience climbing snowy mountains, particularly in the height of winter, but success was imperative to protecting their homeland, so nothing would stop them. Their goal was Tashiro Hot Spring, 20 kilometres south of Aomori City in the Hakkoda Mountains.

The Hakkoda Mountains are a volcanic mountain range consisting of a northern group and southern group of mountains. The highest peak, Mount Odake, reaches 1,585 metres. Much of the range sits in an alpine climate; it's so cold that not even trees are able to grow there.

Locals from Tamogino Village, on the outskirts of Aomori City, advised the unit not to proceed. The men refused to listen to them. The villagers then told them to at the very least hire a guide to take them through the mountains. Again, the men refused. They informed the villagers that they would be just fine with their maps and compasses.

The unit made good progress, but the sleigh corps were falling behind, so the rest of the men stopped to have lunch. The 210-strong unit had with it 14 sleighs, each carrying roughly 80 kg of supplies that needed at least four men to pull. As the men ate lunch, they noticed the weather suddenly changing. A blizzard was starting to blow in. The military physician with the unit, Officer Nagai, recommended the men turn back, and the officers discussed the best course of action. They considered returning; they didn't have enough equipment, and the weather was only going to get worse. But the men wanted to press on, and so they did.

By 4 p.m., the 210-strong unit reached Umatateba, only four kilometres from their objective of Tashiro Hot Spring. Umatateba's peak reaches 732 metres, only half as tall as Mount Odake, but it was the height of winter, and the weather was getting progressively worse. Strong winds. Heavy snow. A blizzard was settling in.

By 5 p.m., the unit decided to abandon the sleighs and split the supplies up amongst the men to carry on foot. Several men were forced to carry the large copper pots the army cooked their food in through the blizzard, making things even rougher.

The recon team was unable to find a path through the blizzard, and only through pure luck were they able to find their way back to the main body of the unit. The officers sent out another team, but the sun was setting and the blizzard worsening, so again they were unable to find a path through to Tashiro. Reluctantly, the men looked for a place to set up shelter for the night.

At 8:15 p.m., the men set up shelter in Hirazawa Forest, only 1.5 kilometres from Tashiro. They dug five trenches roughly 5 metres by 2.5 metres into which 40 men each huddled inside. But the trenches had no covers, and thus no heat insulation. The men weren't even able to sit down.

At 9 p.m., when everyone was in the shelters, the men distributed sticky rice, canned food, and a few blocks of charcoal. But it was not enough for the large number of men in each trench, only allowing one fire that the men had to take turns huddling around.

The soldiers forced to carry the large pots struggled when it came time to cook. They dug for several metres through the snow but were unable to find hard ground. They gave up and put the pots on the snow, but then had trouble getting a fire to light. Once they did, the fire melted the snow, causing the pots to tilt and fall over. By 1 a.m. that night, the men were finally able to distribute half-cooked food from the pots, and they then attempted to heat up some sake in them, but the smell was so bad that no-one could drink it.

The men tried to nap against the walls of their snow trenches, but the temperature dropped to minus 20 degrees Celsius. Trying to avoid frostbite, the men took to singing war songs and were ordered to march on the spot to keep warm. The men were only able to grab less than an hour and a half's sleep at best. They were scheduled to move out at 5 a.m., but the officers complained of the frightful cold, and the men feared frostbite. The officers discussed what they should do and at 2 a.m. on the morning of January 24, the men set out once again.

By 3 a.m., the men found themselves lost in a gorge near Narusawa and were about to turn back to their former shelter site when Sergeant Major Sato said he knew the way to Tashiro. Major Yamaguchi reportedly replied, "If you know the way, then go ahead and show us." But Sergeant Major Sato got lost and instead led them back down the valley towards Komagome River. The men were exhausted and falling out of rank. Major Yamaguchi realised they'd made a grave mistake, and with the blizzard erasing all trace of the path they'd followed to get there, they were completely lost.

The men started to climb the cliff before them to escape the valley. It was here that First Lieutenant Mizuno Tadayoshi of the Fourth Platoon, a man from Tokyo of noble birth, lost consciousness and died from the cold. Unit morale was destroyed.

Once the men reached the top of the cliff, they made their way upstream towards Narusawa, again looking for somewhere to take shelter. But they were in the shade of the mountains; the winds were reaching speeds of 29m/s and the temperature dropped to minus 25 degrees Celsius. Snowfall in the valley reached 6~9 metres, and in these harsh conditions, one-fourth of the unit died. The luggage carriers were amongst the first to go, and the rest of the men were forced to carry the large cooking pots in their stead. By evening, they were told to leave them behind.

The men marched for 14 hours straight, and in the end, their second shelter site in Narusawa was only 700 metres from the first. With their supplies gone and many of the men missing, the remaining soldiers were forced to take shelter in the open. The only food left was what they had on their person, but it had also frozen in the cold and was largely inedible.

The remaining men put those with frostbite in the middle and surrounded them, again singing war songs and marching on the spot to keep warm and distract from their terrible hunger. But the blizzard grew even more fierce, and temperatures dropped to nearly minus 50 degrees Celsius, the coldest ever recorded in Japan's history. Running on empty stomachs with no sleep and having spent two days taking the full force of the coldest blizzard in history without shelter, many of the remaining soldiers died where they stood.

The unit was supposed to return to Aomori on January 24. Men were sent to meet them in Tamogino, on the outskirts of the mountains. They waited until midnight, but there was still no news from the men. Yet they did not set out immediately to find them. Instead, they hoped they would find their way back themselves.

The remains of the unit planned to set out at dawn on the morning of January 25, but the large number of dying men forced them to move again at 3 a.m. They made their way back towards Umatateba. Over 70 men had died or gone missing, and many more were suffering from frostbite. Their compasses were frozen and they were unable to rely upon their maps. The men simply picked a direction and walked.

The men wandered around the mountains, running into obstacle after obstacle. The officers again discussed what to do and decided to dissolve the unit. It would be up to each man to find his own way back. "It would appear that the gods have abandoned us," Captain Kannari told his men.

The men started to go mad. Several removed their clothes and ran around naked. Others threw themselves into the river, claiming it would take them home. Others attacked trees with their bayonets, declaring they would make a raft to carry them back. Unable to do anything with their frozen hands, several men wet themselves and suffered from even more frostbite that eventually led to death.

Another 30 men died in the cold, and even more went missing. Several men under Sergeant Major Hasegawa took shelter in a small charcoal hut after escaping an avalanche. They started a fire for warmth, but fearing they would pass out from their exhaustion and the fire would rage out of control and kill them, they put it out again and suffered in the cold.

The main body of the unit returned to their second shelter site. It was here that Major Yamaguchi fell unconscious and died.

By 7 a.m., the weather was starting to let up, so Captain Kuraishi sent out a team of seven men towards Tamogino for reconnaissance, and six men towards Tashiro. Around 10 a.m., one soldier claimed to see the recon team in the distance.

Captain Kuraishi ordered one of the men to blow the signal trumpet, but his lips froze to it and he had no strength to make any sound to begin with. By 11 a.m. nobody had arrived, and they put down the earlier sighting to wind blowing through the trees. The men were even more demoralised.

The first group of men with Corporal Takahashi found their way back around 11:30 a.m., thanks to Private First Class Sasaki Shimokichi. They informed the remaining soldiers that they had found the way back. They set out at midday; by this point, only 60 or so men of the original 210 were still alive. They arrived in Umatateba at 3 p.m. and waited for the other men to arrive. They never did. Not too long later, both Private First Class Sasaki and Corporal Takahashi lay down together and died.

The rest of the men continued on. By 5 p.m., the sun was gone, and Captain Kuraishi noticed several of his men had lagged behind and gone missing, including one of the doctors who had been doing his best the whole time to lessen the pain the men were in. In the end, he too succumbed to the cold and died. The men were scattered. Captain Kuraishi sent men out to find them, but it was impossible to gather everyone back together again.

Around 11 p.m. that night, Captain Kuraishi set out to find Major Yamaguchi's men. He found them close to midnight and they returned to the bivouac he had set up. The men tried yelling and screaming to stay awake, and setting the packs alight of soldiers who had passed to keep warm, but even more men died from the cold. What happened after that is unclear; of the few men who survived, their recollections of the day following differ.

Back in Aomori, they finally decided to send men out to find the unit. On January 26, 60 soldiers were sent out to find the missing men.

Corporal Goto, along with four or five other men, fell into a stupor due to the cold and lack of food. He awoke on the morning of the 26th and found the weather was clear, but he was alone. A few men were straggling, trying to find the way back, but Goto set out by himself. He climbed to high ground and met up with Captain Kannnari and Second Lieutenant Suzuki, and they pressed on together. The skies were clear and bright. For the first time since they set out, there was no snowfall. The men set up shelter again that night, exhausted. What would take a normal man roughly two hours to cover instead took them the whole day.

On the 27th, the remaining men again split into two groups. Captain Kuraishi's men went towards Komagome River while Captain Kannari's men proceeded forward. Captain Kannari's men faced heavy snowfall once more and several men lost their way. Only four men remained. Second Lieutenant Suzuki said he would seek high ground to see where they were. He never returned. Three men were left, but before long, soldier Oikawa Tokusaburo died. Only Captain Kannari and Corporal Goto were left. They moved on, but then Captain Kannari fell into the snow and didn't get up again. Corporal Goto proceeded by himself.

At 10 a.m. on January 27, the rescue party finally found Corporal Goto standing in the snow. He was the first of only 11 survivors to be found. Rescue workers, soldiers, and villagers worked around the clock for months. The final survivor was found on February 2, while the last body was recovered on May 28.

While Corporal Goto's life was saved, after rescue he had to have his arms and legs amputated as a result of frostbite. Many of the other survivors suffered the same fate. The horrific incident became the largest mountaineering disaster in modern history. 199 men lost their lives in the Hakkoda Mountains over those few days, and it took several months to recover all the bodies. A bronze memorial statue of Corporal Goto was erected close to the area the men were lost in, and the first and second shelter sites now sit just a few hundred metres from each other on a main road.

As you might expect from such a large loss of life in such terrible circumstances, the Hakkoda Mountains thereafter came to be known as haunted. People claimed that if you visited the statue of Corporal Goto at night time, you could hear the death march of the ghostly soldiers who never returned home. To this day, you can still hear them around the statue and tea shop that opened nearby; a place for weary travellers to take a moment of much-needed rest that the Hakkoda soldiers never could.

A TV program from the 1990s set up cameras in front of the bronze statue for a supernatural special. The program aired footage in which they claimed to capture the spirits of several soldiers in front of the statue at night. Dark figures can be seen in front of the statue, but the footage is too dark to clearly see anything. Some people took the footage at face value, claiming it was proof that the soldiers' spirits hadn't moved on. Others claimed it was too dark to determine anything, and could easily have been faked. Either way, the footage brought attention to the site and propelled it into the mind of ghost spot hunters once more.

In the book *Kaidan Hyakumonogatari Shin Mimibukuro The Fourth Night*, a young man recounts a ghostly tale that happened to him while travelling through the Hakkoda mountains. He was driving through the mountains one night when, through the darkness, he heard the sounds of soldiers marching in the distance. He panicked and tried to flee, but the spirits of the soldiers chased him. He was able to escape, but the incident stuck with him. There are rumours that if the spirits follow you, they will follow you all the way home and start to have a destructive effect on your everyday life, however, so best be careful when travelling through the mountains alone at night. Which is generally pretty good advice anyway.

On May 17, 2014, the Aomori fire department head office received a strange phone call. One of the officers answered it, but there was nothing but a strange "buu buu" sound on the other end of the line. They traced the call and found it was coming from a villa in Komagome. A fire truck set out to investigate, but when they got there, they found the villa was empty... So, who called them? The villa was right in the middle of the area the soldiers were lost in all those years ago. Did one finally reach the villa and attempt to call for help? The incident was picked up by the news, and some took this as proof that the spirits are still wandering the mountains, lost and looking for help. Others, however, saw it as just a prank, or perhaps even crossed wires.

In 1977, *Mount Hakkoda*, a film based on the Hakkoda Mountains incident was released. It was based on the documentary novel written by Nitta Jiro and starred popular Japanese actor Takakura Ken. Takakura took his role very seriously, and reportedly said during filming that, "I absolutely will not sit down." Some took this to be nothing more than method acting, getting into the role and attempting to recreate what the real soldiers went through, but there were other rumours as well. Rumours that perhaps the lead actor of *Mount Hakkoda* was possessed by one of the spirits of the dead; a spirit who wished to convey just how much pain the men had been through accurately.

Roughly 12 kilometres from the bronze statue of Corporal Goto, you'll find Jogakura Bridge. The bridge is 122 metres high, looking over the Jogakura Valley and connecting the mountains in the east with the mountains in the west. It was completed in 1995, so the bridge is a rather recent addition to the landscape, but it already comes with its own set of ghost stories as well.

Jogakura Bridge, like many other bridges around the country, is a famous *tobiori*, or jumping, spot. There are two main rumours that circulate about the bridge and its reputation as a supposed suicide spot.

The first rumour states that if you look over the edge of the bridge, you will be pulled down into the depths below. This presumably goes a little further than simple vertigo, with the implication being that the spirits of those who jumped (or were pulled) over the bridge are constantly looking for more people to join them. This isn't exclusive to Jogakura; throughout this book alone you'll find several ghost spots that claim the exact same phenomenon. The spirits love company, and are not opposed to dragging people to their deaths to join them.

The second rumour is another ghost spot staple. Walk across the bridge at night and you'll see ghostly figures. Look over the bridge during the day and they'll try to pull you over, but walk over the bridge at night and you'll instead find them loitering above. Perhaps they're looking for fresh victims? There must surely be fewer people using the bridge in the dark, so perhaps the spirits need a somewhat more direct approach come nightfall.

But some occult fans have suggested that the lack of any solid history, ghost sightings, or stories means that the bridge isn't a real ghost spot. There's nothing in the local newspapers about any suicides at the bridge, so where did it get its reputation? Looking out over the valley from the bridge certainly brings with it a sense of melancholy, and in the past, many people did struggle to traverse the mountains before the bridge was constructed. Perhaps that feeling still lingers, or perhaps it was all made up by people looking to cash in on the ghost spot craze.

One thing is for certain, however. The Hakkoda Mountains are not to be taken lightly, as the very real tragedy that took place there a century ago can attest to.

Memorial Forest

Location: Dai 47 Chiwari, Nishianiwa, Shizukuishi, Iwate District, Iwate Prefecture, 020-0572

Please note that some of the details in this story are rather gruesome. Proceed with caution or skip if you are squeamish.

A group of friends went to the Memorial Forest in Iwate Prefecture while on a bike tour. They went deep into the forest, laughing and joking the whole way. But as they went further in, suddenly the air around them changed. It seemed to grow heavy. Thick. Oppressive.

One of the members suggested they should leave, and everyone was in agreement. Unlike the other places they had visited, this place felt wrong. Dangerous. It was not a place that living beings should be in.

But when they reached the exit, they suddenly realised they were missing someone. It was already late and the forest was pitch black. Not a single person wanted to go back in there again, especially now. They decided to return in the morning. As awful as it was, their friend would have to tough it out for the night without them.

When they returned the next morning, they found the man sitting on his bike, laughing like a madman…

All Nippon Airways Flight 58 left Chitose Airport, near Sapporo, on July 30, 1971. The plane was a Boeing 727-281 with registration JA8329. It was a young plane, not even six months old at the time of takeoff, but its pilot, Kawanishi Saburo (41), was a veteran with over 8,000 hours of flight experience behind him. 155 passengers and seven crew members were on board. Of the passengers, 125 were a tour group from Fuji, Shizuoka Prefecture. They were the members of a society of war-bereaved families for Japanese servicemen killed in World War II, and they were returning home from a tour of scenic Hokkaido. They were scheduled to arrive at Tokyo's Haneda International Airport.

Around the same time, Japan Air Self-Defence Force trainee pilot Technical Sergeant Ichikawa Yoshimi (22) was practising air combat manoeuvring in an F-86F Sabre jet fighter. He had only 21 hours of flight experience behind him, but his instructor was with him in a separate jet. They departed from Matsushima Airbase in Miyagi Prefecture and were in the air above Morioka, the capital city of Iwate Prefecture.

ANA Flight 58 was cruising at an altitude of roughly 8,500 metres. It wasn't a long flight to Tokyo; only roughly an hour and a half. Ichikawa, however, wasn't paying attention to air traffic. Approximately 30 minutes after Flight 58 left Hokkaido, Ichikawa received a message from his instructor to break away; Flight 58 was nearing, and Ichikawa had not seen its approach. He panicked and banked to the left to avoid the large passenger plane, but it was already too late. Ichikawa ejected from his Sabre, but the 162 people aboard the Boeing 727 were not so lucky.

The Sabre's right wing struck the Boeing's left tailplane. The plane entered a steep dive and disintegrated in the air. All on board were killed, making the incident the deadliest air disaster in history at the time. Pieces of the plane landed in Shizukuishi, Iwate Prefecture, in an area of mountainous forest that is now known as *Irei no Mori*, or the Memorial Forest. Pieces of the destroyed aircraft travelled through the air so fast that it was said they could hear the sonic booms all the way over in Morioka City.

But that wasn't the end of the tragedy. Not even close. At the time of the crash, the passenger plane was sitting at roughly 7,900 metres in the air. There were 162 people on board. Every single one of those bodies travelled close to 8,000 metres before hitting the ground. It's not a pleasant thought, but for the people of Shizukuishi, it was a horrific reality. When people looked up into the sky after hearing the sonic booms, they saw the bodies of those on board hurtling at supersonic speed towards the ground. But the bodies didn't just land in the forest. They also landed in the city itself; in people's yards, on the streets, and even in the elementary school grounds.

Volunteers and firefighters worked around the clock to recover the bodies. In what is now the Memorial Forest they found the trees painted red with blood. Bodies and limbs hung from branches and were speared on the trees. Blood-soaked clothes littered the area. It took three days in total to find all the bodies, but the accident took place at the height of summer. Japanese summers are extremely hot and humid. The smell of decomposing corpses in the city was horrific. But it wasn't just the corpses; many of the bodies exploded upon impact, and it was impossible to find all the pieces. The decomposing flesh gave off phosphoric acid, and when the summer rains hit, this caused what is now the Memorial Forest to literally glow with the dead.

Several doctors and nurses in the area were tasked with piecing the dead back together. The deceased deserved to be mourned as people, not 'things.' Despite the living hell the city became, many medical workers also worked around the clock identifying bodies and trying to put them back together. Their families wouldn't be able to properly mourn them otherwise.

As you might expect from such a horrific tragedy, the Memorial Forest quickly became the subject of hauntings and ghostly rumours. There wasn't a person around who didn't know of it, and particularly for the locals, it was one of the most famous ghost spots around.

One story tells of a young man who, after being rejected by a woman he liked, abducted her and took her to the Memorial Forest. He tied her to a tree and left her there overnight to teach her a lesson. When he returned the next day, however, he found that she was dead, and her hair had turned completely white. True or not, the story spread, and rumours that the forest was haunted were further strengthened.

Another rumour states that if you drive past the

forest, bloody handprints will appear on the car bonnet or front windscreen. Yet another legend tells of the time five people went to visit the forest, but one of them disappeared... only to be found crippled in the mountains of Akita over 100km away a few days later.

Shizukuishi holds various festivals each year, but when they do, police patrol the entrance of the forest so rowdy teenagers can't enter for *kimodameshi*, or tests of courage. Why? Because it's too dangerous. Not just because it's a dark forest, but because of the spirits that linger there, unable to move on after such a horrific tragedy.

Despite how well known the Memorial Forest is, it rarely appears on TV. Japan loves taking entertainers and spirit mediums to various haunted locations during the hot summer months, and there are endless programs dedicated to exploring Japan's spookiest spots. But they rarely visit the Memorial Forest. Some people have suggested that this is because, unlike other ghost spots in Japan, this one is actually haunted. After such a tragedy, how could it not be? But others have suggested that because such a real tragedy took place there, that is exactly why people don't go there for fun. Families of the people who died in the accident are still alive today. It's not a place to visit for entertainment.

Young Lady's Prayer

Location: Nishinohama 79-8, Isozaki, Matsushima-machi, Miyagi District, Miyagi Prefecture, 981-0212

In a forest in Miyagi Prefecture, there stands a tree. Carved into the trunk of that tree are the final words of a young woman who took her own life. They say that anyone who reads the "Young Lady's Prayer" will be cursed to die as well.

Undeterred, a young man set out to find the tree. The first time, he was unsuccessful; there are a lot of trees in the forest, after all, and the sheer cliffs make the area dangerous to explore. But the second time, lady luck shined upon him. He found the Young Lady's Prayer.

Cigarette butts littered the ground. It was an unwritten rule that, instead of leaving incense, you were to leave smokes as a gift to the young lady's spirit. The young man didn't smoke and struggled to light the cigarette, but he persevered. He didn't want to upset her, after all.

The words stood before him. The girl carved out a large section of trunk before carving her final message to the world. They were a strange mix of Chinese characters and *katakana*, a script generally used for writing foreign words. Trying to read the combination was both off-putting and difficult. Not only that, the words themselves were puzzling. What was the girl trying to say?

The young man left his offerings to the girl and

got up to leave. He was satisfied that he finally found the tree and he was able to read her final message firsthand. But as he turned around to go home, he felt something brush the back of his head, like a hand running across his hair. No, it wasn't a touch. It was more like something grabbing at him. Tugging on his hair. He turned back. There was nobody else there but him…

In 1967, a female high school student was found hanging from a tree in Miyagi Prefecture with a mysterious message carved into its bark.

> "At this time, I have realised my limit.
> I have lost all meaning to exist with nature.
> Holding death in my hands,
> I will overcome this.
> Showa Year 42, Eldest Son."

What the girl was trying to convey with her final words remains a mystery. Why did she sign it with the Chinese characters for "eldest son"? Why did she use a combination of Chinese characters and katakana, making the words extremely difficult to read? It's possible, of course, that she carved her message in katakana, rather than the standard *hiragana* script, because hiragana is curved and thus more difficult to carve, but the end result was foreign and off-putting nevertheless.

People have spent years trying to find the hidden meaning behind her final words. Some have suggested the girl didn't carve the message at all; the message is unrelated and that just happened to be the tree she picked. Others have said that the characters used for "eldest son" at the end of the message were actually meant to signify her boyfriend. In reality, she was so heartbroken by boy troubles that she took her own life. The true answer is that we'll never know; all we have are the remains of a message that was carved over 50 years ago, but that won't keep people from speculating on what really happened.

One of the rules for visiting the Young Lady's Prayer, if you can find the tree, is to leave cigarettes as an offering. Nobody knows how this rule came about, but over the years it became the accepted thing to do. To this day, mountains of cigarette butts surround the remains of the tree the young lady hung herself from.

The original tree was, at some point, cut down, and perhaps unsurprisingly, the stump is now little more than burnt remains, likely from a rogue cigarette butt that wasn't put out. The carved message remains, however. The section of tree was cut down and now lies a few metres away on the ground, deteriorating, but still legible over 50 years later.

Over the years, a legend sprung up that said anyone who reads the Young Lady's Prayer would be cursed to die as well. Considering pictures of the tree and its message are all over the internet, this seems highly unlikely, but it's possible this legend grew out of another real-life tragedy.

A female announcer from Miyagi Prefecture visited the site to film a report for a local TV channel, but on her way back she was involved in an accident with a truck and died. Ever since that incident, visits to the tree decreased dramatically, but its legend continued to grow.

It's difficult to say how much longer the tree will be around. The original stump has already been burnt to the ground thanks to the carelessness of those who visit it, and it's possible that if people aren't careful in the future, the Young Lady's Prayer may be the next to go.

Kurozuka

Location: 4 Chome Adachigahara, Nihonmatsu, Fukushima Prefecture, 964-0938

It was the year of the fire tiger in the Jinki Era (726). A monk from the Kii Province, Tokobo Yukei, was travelling through Adachigahara. The sun was setting, so he stopped by a cavern to request shelter for the night. An old woman lived inside. The old woman kindly invited him in. She told Yukei that she didn't have enough firewood, so she would go out to gather some more. But while she was gone, he was not to look in the back room.

But Yukei was overcome with curiosity, and after she left, he peeked into the room. There he found a mountain of human bones piled high. Shocked, Yukei remembered hearing a story of an *onibaba* who killed travellers in Adachigahara and ate their flesh. Suspecting the old woman was that onibaba, he fled the cavern.

The old woman returned a short while later, and when she noticed Yukei fleeing, she ran after him with incredible speed. A terrifying look on her face, she soon caught up to him. Driven into a corner, Yukei took out his statue of Nyoirin Kannon out of his luggage and frantically began to pray. Then, the statue started to float in the air before him. It formed a white bow of light with the power to exorcise demons, and from it shot forth an arrow made of vajra. The onibaba was vanquished.

Although she was defeated, the onibaba was able to enter heaven with the guidance of the Kannon statue. Yukei built a mound on the shores of the Abukuma River to bury her, and after that it became known as Kurozuka, the black mound. The statue that guided the onibaba to heaven was thereafter called the White Bow Kannon, and it took on deep faith...

The above is the legend told about Kurozuka, the grave of an onibaba that you can visit in Fukushima Prefecture. 100 metres away you can visit the Kanzeji Temple, which is said to also have been built by Yukei to deify Nyoirin Kannon. The temple grounds house the cavern where the onibaba lived, and the pond is said to be where she washed her blood-soaked knife (also called the Blood Pond). That's not the only story told about the onibaba of Adachigahara, however. There's another, more sinister tale of how the onibaba came to be.

There was once a wet nurse called Iwate who worked for the Imperial Court in Kyoto. One day, the princess she was caring for fell sick to a mysterious illness. But no matter what they tried, nothing worked, and so Iwate went to see a famous fortuneteller.

"If you feed her the liver of a live pregnant woman, she will get better," the fortuneteller said.

But it was not so easy to find a pregnant woman, nor was getting the liver from a live one so easy to come by. Leaving her own daughter behind to find what she needed, Iwate eventually found herself all the way in Adachigahara, where she set up house next to a cave.

One day, a young man by the name of Ikomanosuke, and his wife Koi, lost their way and appeared by Iwate's cave. They were on a trip, looking for Koi's mother. They requested to stay the night in Iwate's cavern, but that night, Koi went into labour.

Ikomanosuke hurried to find a doctor, but on the way he suddenly felt like something was wrong, so he returned to the cave. When he got there, he found Koi on the edge of death at Iwate's hand. Driven mad with despair, Ikomanosuke drove his own sword through his stomach to join his wife in the afterlife.

Iwate then pulled a talisman from Koi's kimono. It was the same talisman she had given her own daughter when she left Kyoto all those years ago. She had killed her own daughter. Realising this, Iwate went mad and transformed into the fearsome onibaba. Whenever travellers came to stay in her cavern for the night, she would kill them and consume their flesh…

Although it's no longer haunted by the onibaba, it's said that if you injure yourself by falling from the cavern she once lived in, the wounds will refuse to heal. Children often play in the temple grounds, and the cavern is just the right height for kids to climb upon, and then fall from. Care must be taken, for while the onibaba is gone, danger still lurks where she once lived.

There is also a museum on the temple grounds, and inside you can view the actual knife that it's said the onibaba used to kill her victims, as well as the pot she used to boil them, and the hoe she used to bury their remains.

In contrast to most modern ghost spots, Kurozuka holds a long history reaching back almost 1,300 years. While you might not run into any modern ghosts who were violently murdered, you can get a glimpse into an equally brutal past, a closer look into an important piece of Japanese folklore, and view the birthplace of a gruesome legend.

KANTO

Kasumigaura Branch Hospital

Location: 2020 Oyama, Miho, Inashiki District, Ibaraki Prefecture, 300-0402

At the end of that road is another world.

That's what they said about Kasumigaura Branch Hospital, an abandoned building at the end of Prefectural Road 120 in Ibaraki Prefecture. It was once a naval base during the Second World War, then it was reborn as a medical college, and finally, it became an abandoned shell of a building with more bad memories than good.

For an abandoned building, security was tight. The building was surrounded by wire fencing, the windows boarded up, and light sensors attached to alert the police of intruders. Why go to all that trouble for an empty building? It was suspicious. But if you believed the rumours, it was for good reason.

There were ghosts in there, and they weren't happy. The ghosts were so powerful that they could affect the lives of people who stepped into their space, even when they were gone. But to one young man and his friend, they weren't going to let that stop them. Mostly, anyway.

He wasn't brave enough to actually go into the building, so he stood by the fence and took pictures. As he was snapping away, he noticed his friend trembling beside him.

"What's wrong?" he asked. But he could get no coherent answer from him. His friend just continued to mutter the word "window" over and over. The young man looked up at the window, but he couldn't see anything there.

Unsure of what to do, but fearing that he might be next to see whatever invisible force had grabbed his friend, he grabbed him by the arm and forcibly dragged him away.

It wasn't until they saw the lights of civilisation that they stopped, and with tears in his eyes, the young man's friend told him about what he saw. In the crack between the window frame and the boards covering it, he saw a ghost pass by. And that ghost was looking down at them…

These days, Kasumigaura Branch Hospital can be found in an otherwise desolate and empty landscape close to Kasumigaura Bay in Ibaraki prefecture. Surrounded by little more than a solar power generation facility and a boat parking lot, the area was once used by the Imperial Navy before a branch of the Tokyo Medical and Dental College was built there. Now, the husk of the building remains abandoned and fenced off to the public.

The building is famous within Ibaraki prefecture as a *haikyo*, or abandoned building, but it's also come to be famous country-wide as a ghost spot as well. It is, potentially, the only public hospital in Japan to have been built on a former naval base.

From the outside, the building looks like a large Western lodging and has been cordoned off with a metal fence and barbed wire forbidding people to enter. Yet one section of the fence close to the entrance has been cut down, allowing entry to the many ghost hunters and thrill seekers who visit the former branch hospital each year.

Over 1,000 soldiers worked at the Imperial Naval Port during the Second World War. Seaplane crew members in particular were trained in the area, and the building that was to become Kasumigaura Branch Hospital was used as the flying corps headquarters. Then, in 1946, when the war was over, the Tokyo Medical and Dental College university hospital moved in and used the building to treat tuberculosis patients. It remained open until 1997, when it was then abandoned and left to reach its current state.

As with many other ghost spots around the country, Kasumigaura Branch Hospital was first featured in the popular ghost video series *Honto ni Atta! Noroi no Video*. While it was known locally as a ghost spot and a place to test one's courage, this series introduced the former hospital to occult-lovers all over the country. Locals claimed that you could see the spirits of soldiers and nurses who died during the war, although nobody ever came forward saying that they themselves had seen such spirits. As such, some came to view the abandoned hospital's reputation as a ghost spot as a mere fabrication of the media.

And yet, if you ask the locals these days if Kasumigaura Branch Hospital is haunted, most will answer yes. Even if it wasn't haunted by the spirits of soldiers and nurses who died during the war, later ghosts did take up residence in the building. The negative energy of locations related to war remains over the years, stagnating and surging over a long period of time before activating at a later date. While it may not have been haunted then, it is now, or so they say.

People have claimed to see black shadowy figures inside, and the *Honto ni Atta!* video also claimed to have captured a ghost on video that was missing his head. Some have tried to explain the ghost as a war prisoner who was subject to inhumane experimentation during the war. Other strange experiences within the building include the sensation of being touched on the neck or shoulders, and those who enter the building as a joke can end up going insane.

Some have said that they discovered an unknown woman sitting in the back of their car when driving away from the building, and others claim there is a woman in a white dress in one of the rooms on the second floor. If you see her, then you are almost certain to have an accident on your way home. There are even rumours of a door within the building that cannot be opened by any means.

In 1994, Japanese pop group Spitz released a music video for their song "Sora mo Toberu Hazu." The video was filmed at Kasumigaura Branch Hospital, and it became a topic of conversation amongst occult-lovers thanks to a scene around the 4:16 mark. An old man with a cane is standing in front of a few broken windows out the rear of the building. In the window directly behind him, a white shadow can be seen moving and disappearing behind the wall. Many claim that the music video managed to capture one of the several spirits still residing in the building. You can watch the video on

YouTube and judge for yourself.

There are plans to turn the building into a national science museum in the future, so it may not remain a ghost spot for much longer. Or perhaps the science museum will instead take on the negative energy that is said to lurk there.

Hotaka Shrine

Location: Azumachokusagi, Midori, Gunma Prefecture, 376-0302

The young couple were just there for a bit of fun. They heard the Hotaka Shrine was abandoned and wanted to see it for themselves firsthand. Who knew, they might even find something interesting there? Perhaps some old shrine goods left inside the building, or even better, one of the ghosts said to inhabit the area. At least, that was what the young man was hoping for. His girlfriend, however, was less keen on the idea. But she didn't want to be left alone in the car, so she grabbed her camera and joined him.

The shrine was overgrown with weeds and, at first glance, kind of creepy. Her boyfriend rushed ahead, ignoring her pleas to slow down. She didn't want to be there. She was scared, and something about the place set her nerves on edge. But no matter how much she complained and begged to get out of there, her boyfriend refused to listen.

He grabbed the shrine doors and tugged. They refused to open. He moved over to the windows and peeked inside instead. She begged him, over and over. She could feel someone—or something—looking at her. It unnerved her.

"Come on, quit it! Let's go!"

Finally, he relented, and she swung the camera around to return to the car. It wasn't until later when she was watching what she recorded that she noticed an old woman standing behind the pillar, staring intensely at her...

Hotaka Shrine was built in its current location in Azumachokusagi, Gunma Prefecture, in 1973. However, it eventually closed to the public sometime around 2000. It sits close to Kusaki Lake, a man-made lake that was created after the nearby Kusaki Dam finished construction in 1976. The shrine is surrounded by mountains and forest, and the only things you'll find nearby are the Kotsune Temple, an art museum, and a few residential houses. With an ageing population and many of the residents moving to bigger cities, the area is progressively becoming less populated and thus it's thought the shrine fell into ruin.

There are two concrete shrine gates that lead to the main building, which sits high behind a large concrete fence much like a castle. A "no trespassing" sign and steel fence have been placed at the stair entrance to keep the public out. The shrine gates still show evidence of maintenance and weeding, so the building hasn't been entirely abandoned. At the very least, the front is kept neat and tidy, even though the main building has been marked off-limits to all.

It is, of course, very easy to jump over the small fence placed at the foot of the stair entrance, so many *haikyo* hunters over the years have been inside and photographed the remains of the shrine for all to see. The inside is, for the most part, empty, although for some reason a large Japanese drum alone remains. There have long been rumours of people hearing the sound of a drum coming from the shrine despite the fact no-one is around at the time. Perhaps the spirits are also unable to resist a good beat every now and then.

One theory, aside from the depopulation of the surrounding suburbs, gives another reason for why Hotaka Shrine closed down and is so disliked by spirit mediums.

In 1977, the nearby Kusaki Dam was finished. In order to build the dam, several villages that were located in the nearby valley had to be abandoned. There was even a railway line with a small station; Kusaki Station. The station, like the villages, was abandoned, and now they all sit at the bottom of the lake.

Yet when there is a water shortage, the ruins at the bottom of the man-made lake resurface, and every now and then you can still see them when the water dries up. You can also find the remains of a shrine that is rumoured to be the predecessor of Hotaka Shrine before it was moved. Perhaps the spirits are upset with the move, and upset that their homes now sit at the bottom of a lake.

In 2007, *Honto ni Atta! Noroi no Video 23* (Real Cursed Videos) was released, featuring Hotaka Shrine in one of its stories. In the video, a young couple went to visit Hotaka Shrine for *kimodameshi*, a test of courage. They were filming each other when one of them managed to capture a ghost in the background of the shot. The ghost was of an old woman. On their way home, they mysteriously died in a traffic accident. Rumour has it the old woman died on that same road.

The shrine was also featured in 2016 on the

show *Kano Eiko no Iku to Shinu Kamoshirenai Kimodameshi Fuyu no Jin* (Tests of Courage That May Kill You With Kano Eiko, Winter Encampment). The show featured comedian Kano visiting various ghost spots around the country with two spirit mediums in tow. When they arrived at the shrine they found the second shrine gate destroyed, and the mediums claimed the area was full of spirits. After a brief exploration inside the main shrine building, the mediums judged the area too dangerous and everyone was forced to leave. No explanation was given as to why, but one of the mediums claimed the area had seen many disasters over the years, and they weren't alone in the building.

The original video from *Honto ni Atta* also featured on an episode of *Sekai no Kowai Yoru* (Scary Nights from Around the World) in 2014. Three comedians from the show were sent to investigate the abandoned shrine themselves, with one of the men sitting alone inside the building with a camera. The man claimed to capture a recording of footsteps and a drum beating before freaking out and fleeing the building. A medium on set made all three men pray and apologise before they could leave. He claimed a spirit was trying to communicate with them in the only way it knew how.

Being a small countryside shrine, there's not a lot of solid information about Hotaka. This lack of information and constant appearances on TV shows and DVDs has helped it become a popular spot for ghost hunters, however.

Chichibu Lake Suspension Bridge

Location: National Highway 140, Otaki, Chichibu City, Saitama Prefecture, 369-1901

"It's beautiful, isn't it? A place like this, situated between two mountains out in the wild, it might be calm, but it's a great place for spirits to gather."

That's what the man told his two assistants as they looked out over Chichibu Lake Suspension Bridge for the first time. The man was famous for his ability to see ghosts, and they were there to record some footage for a ghost special.

"This bridge is the last thing many people ever see. It leads to another world."

He sent one of his assistants across the bridge with a camera so she could experience it for herself. The woman also had a strong ability to sense the supernatural, but when she reached the halfway point, she suddenly stopped. She was overcome with a feeling of unease. If she went any further, something terrible would happen. She could sense the spirit of a woman who had killed herself on that very spot. Fearing what would happen if she stayed there any longer, she quickly returned to solid land.

The man sent his second assistant across the bridge. This woman had no experience with the supernatural, but as she reached the same spot as the first assistant, she stopped. She was scared, but more than that, she was sad. Lonely. She understood the desire one might have to throw themselves into the cold waters below and end everything, because she felt it too. Drawing her to the bridge's edge. Was the spirit of the woman still lingering in this world, looking for help to move on, or was it something more sinister, looking for fresh souls to drag down...?

Chichibu Lake Suspension Bridge is located in Chichibu City in Saitama Prefecture. It's a small pedestrian bridge about 200 metres long with a one-metre high wire fence on either side, connecting National Highway 140 with the forest on the other side. It crosses over Chichibu Lake, an artificial lake created thanks to the nearby Futase Dam which was completed in 1961. Due to rock slides on the opposing shore, however, the other side of Chichibu Lake Suspension Bridge is now off-limits, and there is a sign informing people as much. Thanks to that, the bridge is rarely used these days, and while some people still use it to fish in the lake below, there's nowhere to go once you reach the other side. All paths are blocked off.

The site first gained attention after being introduced in Inagawa Junji's *Kyoufu no Genba* (Terrifying Locations) video series in 2003. Inagawa, a famous talent in Japan known for his ability to see ghosts, went with two women to visit the bridge, known as a famous suicide spot to the locals. The three of them claimed they could see the ghost of a female about halfway down, although they were unable to capture her on video. They claimed she was around 20-years-old, wearing old-fashioned clothes and entirely black.

The story goes that, sometime in the past, a young woman was lured to the middle of the bridge by her lover and one of her friends. They then threw her over the edge, and ever since then, she's been known to appear on the same spot she was thrown from, or for those unfortunate enough to look over the edge, she will try to drag them into the water below with her.

Another reason the bridge became a well-known haunted location was because of a very real suicide involving five men and one woman who gassed themselves in their car nearby. On the morning of March 10, 2006, police received a call of a suspicious car by a forest road near Otaki. Inside, they found five men and one woman, all dead without any external injuries. Three were sitting in the front seats and three in the back.

The windows to the car had been covered in black film, and only the passenger's side door was unlocked. The police found charcoal inside the vehicle, leading them to conclude that it was a mass suicide. It was later discovered the six people, all in their 20s, drugged themselves with sleeping pills and alcohol before gassing the car. The incident was picked up by the media and word of the bridge as a suicide spot once again spread countrywide.

Inagawa Junji has claimed that Chichibu Lake has the power to lure people to their doom, and there have been reports of further suicides at the bridge. Although there is no sign like that in Aokigahara Forest warning people to think of their family, and contact help if they are feeling suicidal, you can occasionally find flowers decorating the entrance and various spots along the bridge, honouring the spirits of those who have passed.

As the bridge grew in notoriety, more and more ghost hunters went to visit the site in person. Some have claimed that white hands have reached out to grab them while walking across, while others have claimed that they could hear voices.

But Chichibu Suspension Bridge isn't the only haunted location around Chichibu City. The area is known for up to eight different ghost spots, mostly located around dams, lakes and cliffs in the area. Hanuda Village in the *Siren* video game series is said to be based on an abandoned village found in Chichibu City called Shiraiwa, located roughly 20km from Chichibu Suspension Bridge. You can watch a video that a camera crew shot of the area on YouTube.

On April 22, 2017, an 18-year-old university student drove his car through a guardrail in Chichibu City and crashed 15 metres to the ground below. The driver died while his three passengers survived with major injuries. One of the passengers later told police that "it felt like we hit something, and then the driver's side airbag opened and he couldn't see."

The reason they were even on the road, according to him, was to visit a famous ghost spot nearby. They were touring the many famous haunted locations in the area, and some have claimed that the car crashed because of a *jibakurei* in the area. Jibakurei are the spirits of the dead who are attached to a particular place or item, and due to the nefarious circumstances surrounding their death, are unable to move on to the afterlife. They hang around on earth, dragging more people to their death until the spirit can somehow be appeased. With how many haunted locations can be found around Chichibu City, including perhaps the most infamous of all, Chichibu Suspension Bridge, it's not too hard to see why people might think that.

Yui Grand Hotel

Location: Yui 258, Togane, Chiba Prefecture, 283-0804

A group of friends travelled to the Yui Grand Hotel looking for some fun. The hotel was abandoned and supposedly haunted. Situated in the middle of nowhere, it seemed the perfect spot to waste some time.

They chatted and joked as they walked up the path towards the building, but as they got closer, one of the men stopped dead in his tracks.

"I don't want to go inside," he said. "I can't move my right arm."

He was holding it with his left hand, a scared expression on his face.

"What do you mean, you can't-" Another young man stepped forward and grabbed his arm, but no matter how much he pulled, he couldn't move it. Something was holding it firmly in place.

Feeling uneasy, the man left his scared friend behind and went into the building with everyone else. They climbed the narrow stairs to the second floor, but something on the left side of the building creeped them out, so they entered a room on the right instead.

There was a bed and various other items scattered all over the floor. They looked around, shining the flashlight on anything they could find, but then suddenly it went out. It was a brand new flashlight…

Feeling even more uneasy, the group returned

outside. Their friend's arm still refused to move. Then he looked up at the second floor and indicated something with his chin.

"That second room from the end there... It gives me the creeps. There's something wrong with that place."

The men left the girls behind and went back into the building to check it out. The girls refused and decided to stay back with the other guy.

The men climbed the stairs once more and slowly made their way down the hall. With each step the air seemed to grow thicker and heavier. It was becoming more difficult to proceed.

The group stopped roughly two metres from the room their friend indicated. It wasn't by choice; they were unable to move, frozen on the spot. Paralysis... The group had been to numerous ghost spots over the years, but it was the first time something like this had ever happened, and to so many people at once, no less.

"Shit!" one of them screamed. "Let's get out of here!"

Everyone was in agreement and they turned back. They couldn't run; the staircase was narrow, and there were five of them together. It wouldn't do anyone any good if someone was to get injured, so they walked back as fast as they could without running.

But the young man who tried to help his friend suddenly sensed something from behind. It wasn't a gaze; he didn't feel like someone was looking at them as they retreated. Instead, it was like looking over the edge of a tall building, and something approaching from behind. That was the best way he could put it.

The moment they hit the bottom of the stairs, the men were in silent agreement. They bolted out of the building...

The Yui Grand Hotel can be found just a few short kilometres away from the Pacific Ocean in Togane, Chiba prefecture. It is one of the most well-known ghost spots in Japan thanks to the violent nature of the crime that took place there over ten years ago. Some even call it "the scariest ghost spot in all of Eastern Japan."

The building started business as a hotel in 1975. While there isn't a lot of information remaining about the hotel, many have surmised that it was a love hotel. If not originally, then it turned into one later. The insides of the hotel were gaudily decorated, and at first sight not unlike what you would see in current love hotels.

The location of the hotel was not prime, however. It was hidden way out in the forest, far from any large cities or tourist locations. Its position and difficulty of access meant that in 1995, the hotel went out of business, and it reopened as a live seafood restaurant instead. This gave the building its current nickname, Hotel Katsugyo (live fish and shellfish). The word *katsugyo* can be found in large letters on the sign hanging from the entrance today.

Yet the restaurant was not profitable either, presumably for the same reasons the hotel wasn't. The owners changed tactics again, going back to their original idea and this time turning the building into a motel. But as the saying goes, they kept treading on the same rake, and the motel shortly went out of business as well. The building was abandoned.

As with most abandoned buildings, the Hotel Katsugyo became a well-known local ghost spot. People claimed that when the hotel was in business, a woman was stabbed to death by her partner during an argument in one of the rooms. After that, a string of suicides in the hotel were the real reason for its downfall.

Youngsters were drawn to the building thanks to its novelness. It was clearly the remains of a love hotel with all sorts of lurid rumours about its past, but the giant *KATSUGYO* sign indicated it was a live fish restaurant as well. They weren't two businesses you would expect to see sharing the same space. But it wasn't until a terrible incident took place on December 22, 2004, that the abandoned building became known as a ghost spot country-wide.

Takanaka (17), a female high school student, was hanging out with her friends on the evening of December 21, 2004. On her way home early the next morning, on the 22nd, she bumped into an old friend from junior high. The two young women were seen chatting and catching up by another student (16) who was entering a karaoke bar at the time. When she left, the student saw the old friend talking to police in front of the store. She had reportedly been walking with Takanaka near the south entrance of Mobara Station when they turned a corner and five young men grabbed Takanaka from behind. Scared, her friend ran off, but she recalled Takanaka screaming "stop!" as the men dragged her away.

The men were part of a 'colour gang,' groups of street kids who wore the same colour clothing to imitate street gangs from America. The gang members ranged in age from 16 to 20. Two of them were adults at the time of the crime, and three were juveniles.

The men pushed Takanaka down and stole her money. They then bundled her into a car and drove her to the abandoned Hotel Katsugyo. When they arrived, the men took her inside and strangled her to death with a power cord. They did so because she had seen their faces and could identify them to the police. They then put her body inside a refrigerator that had been left behind in the building and fled. The perpetrators were eventually caught, but ever since then, it's been said that Takanaka's malice remains in the building where she was so brutally killed.

While the building is somewhat out of the way, there is nothing restricting people from exploring the inside (except perhaps the ghosts that are said to haunt it). Nature has started to reclaim the outside of the building, but inside you can still find relics of the former hotel and restaurant. You can see first-hand the tacky paint jobs on the rooms, the gaudy decorations, and leftover spas. Most of the doors and windows have been torn out or destroyed and the walls are covered in graffiti and messages from *haikyo* hunters of times passed.

The hotel was featured on the July 16, 2014

episode of *Sekai no Kowai Yoru Manatsu ni Fueru Zekkyo SP* (Scary World Nights Screams That Tremble in Midsummer SP). Actor Shinoyama Akinobu visited the hotel with a medium, who claimed a spirit was looking down at them from one of the windows on the second floor. The episode became a hot topic after it aired from those who remembered the incident over 10 years earlier, and it helped bring the Yui Grand Hotel back into the mind of the general public once more.

Yahashira Cemetery

Location: 48-2 Tanaka Shinden, Matsudo, Chiba Prefecture, 270-2255

They were out for a midnight drive, and they soon found themselves outside Yahashira Cemetery. One of the most haunted cemeteries in Japan, if you believed the stories. They were near the infamous Section 13, supposedly the most haunted section of the entire cemetery. You never knew what might go down there, but it was never good, like the number suggested.

There were three of them in the car that night. One sat in the driver's seat, another in the passenger's seat, and one more in the back. But for the two sitting in the front, the air suddenly felt strange. Like someone had sat down between them.

They turned the car off to chat, ignoring the strange sensation, when suddenly the person in the back screamed.

"What? What?" they asked.

"My foot! Something grabbed my foot!"

The pair in the front looked down. There were two white hands gripped tightly around their friend's ankles. They looked at each other with wide eyes and screamed. They burst out of the car and ran as fast as their legs would carry them, leaving their friend behind in the back seat, ghostly tendrils wrapped around his legs.

Yet when they returned a short while later, having regained *most* of their composure, they found their friend was nowhere to be seen. In fact, after that night, they never saw him again…

Cemeteries are a beloved location for ghost hunters. It makes sense. If you want to find ghosts, where better to look than the place where the dead are buried? Japan is no exception to this, and the Yahashira Cemetery in Matsudo City, Chiba Prefecture, is one such cemetery that's seen its fair share of hauntings.

Open from 7:30 a.m. to 5:30 p.m. every day, the easiest way to access Yahashira Cemetery is to take the JR East Japan Musashino Line to Shin-Yahashira Station. Take the south exit and then take the Shinkeisei Bus on platform one bound for Higashi-Matsudo Station or Kamishikishako, either of which will drop you off at Yahashira Cemetery Mae, a five-minute walk away. Or, if you'd rather enjoy your time, you could walk straight from Shin-Yahashira station and forgo the bus entirely. The cemetery is only 1.5 km, or roughly a 20-minute walk, away.

Yahashira Cemetery opened on July 1, 1935, and is roughly one square kilometre in size. That's the same size as about 20 Tokyo Domes, so it takes up quite a bit of prime real estate. The *Tokyo Cemetery Stroll* website describes the cemetery as "built in the valley of several slightly elevated knolls with a cheerful atmosphere." From the front gate you can take a peaceful stroll around the French geometry-styled gardens, and enjoy the scenery, such as the water tower that is shaped like a two-storied Buddhist tower.

As is common with other parks and cemeteries

around the country, you can enjoy the cherry blossoms in the park during spring, and the Japanese maple leaves during autumn. The park is also famous for its Japanese red pines, black pines, and Japanese zelkovas. The nearby elementary and junior high schools also use the cemetery for school trips, marathons, and as a walking course for school events.

Famous people buried in the cemetery include Saijo Yaso, who you may remember as the poet who wrote "Tomino's Hell," the supposedly cursed poem. Judo practitioner and educator Kano Jigoro and popular singer Matsuyama Keiko are also buried in the park. But, if you believe the rumours, not all the spirits of those laid to rest in the cemetery have moved on. Rumours of ghosts have been around since at least the 1960s, and the cemetery was also featured on TV as a popular ghost spot.

"There's a female ghost standing beneath the sign in Section 13."

"You can see the ghosts of a young couple sitting on a bench in Section 13."

"There's a male ghost wearing a suit that stands in front of his grave and motions for you to come closer."

"If you visit Section 13, the ghosts of those who have no-one to tend their graves will follow you home."

"If you see the shadow of a figure near the sudden curve on the way to Section 13, that means you'll have an accident on your way home."

"There's a female ghost in Section 4." "A

woman hung herself from one of the trees, and afterwards it was marked with tape. If you happen to find that tree, you'll be cursed."

"There's a cursed bridge, and if you happen to look over the edge while you're crossing it, then…"

There are a wealth of rumours about the ghosts you can encounter at Yahashira Cemetery, but you may have noticed that many of them have something in common. Section 13, and to a lesser extent, Section 4, appear to be the main places that ghosts are likely to appear. Both sections are close to the entrance; Section 4 lies just to the right, and Section 13 is a little further down to the left. But why these two particular sections?

Look at the numbers again. Section 13 will probably be immediate to those who grew up in the West. 13 is an unlucky number, and often associated with the dead. But what about 4? Well, that's Japan's unlucky number, thanks to it possessing the same pronunciation as the word for death. Unlucky Eastern 4 and Unlucky Western 13. Seems like a superstitious no-brainer, right? Not only that, Section 4 houses a crypt, while Section 13 sits close to a reservoir (and we know how much Japanese ghosts love their water). They're the perfect breeding grounds for ghosts.

Yahashira Cemetery is a popular place for kids to try out *kimodameshi*, or tests of courage. On the internet, you can find countless reports of people who visited the cemetery late at night only to run into one of the infamous ghosts detailed above, or regaling their fellow anonymous friends with tales of grizzly accidents they had after visiting the cemetery half-cocked.

Yet, if you remember the cemetery's opening hours from earlier, things might start to seem a little more suspicious. That's right. The cemetery closes at 5.30 p.m. every day. Even during the dead of winter, that's only just barely darkness. Is it possible that these anonymous posters on the internet have just been sneaking into the cemetery after dark, jumping the locked gates to try to find ghosts? Of course. It wouldn't be the first time ghost hunters have trespassed when looking for a thrill. But it's also highly unlikely that most of these stories are from people willing to break the law just for internet brownie points.

The Yahashira Cemetery open and close times came into effect roughly 10 years ago. There was reportedly an increase in crime in the area, and businessmen in particular were under attack by violent youths. In response, the cemetery decided to close early in an effort to keep people safe. It's possible that many of the stories being passed around today of ghosts seen late in the night are simply copy and pastes from 10 years ago. But then again, maybe that's not quite the full story either.

In 2012, filmmaker and author Mori Tatsuya released a book called *Occult*. In the book, he details his visits to various places around Japan that are famous for supernatural phenomena, and one of the places he visits is Yahashira Cemetery.

He learnt of the cemetery from a man he calls H-san, a colleague who grew up in the area. Mori then describes his attempts to visit the cemetery with a man named Akiyama. Akiyama has a strong *reikan*, that is, the ability to see the supernatural. Yet even reaching the cemetery proves difficult for the pair, as their car navigation goes awry and ends up getting them there long after closing hours. Was that a sign that they shouldn't be there? Undeterred, the men stood on the road outside and looked in; there's nothing separating the cemetery from the outside world other than a metre high steel fence, after all.

"There's a soldier." Akiyama pointed out a ghost standing beyond the trees. "Everyone's wearing military uniforms, but not from the Second World War. They're older than that. Maybe the First World War. They're clean. Sabres are hanging from their hips. Are they the army?"

Mori reports that it was around 7 p.m. when they arrived.

"You mean, there are ghosts here right now?" Mori asked his friend.

"There are."

"Soldiers?"

While Mori was unable to see any ghosts himself, Akiyama asserted, without hesitation, that there were ghosts visible to him just beyond the fence. For anyone who possessed a strong reikan, they didn't need to go inside the cemetery to see the ghosts. They were clearly visible from the road outside.

H-san, Mori's colleague who told him about Yahashira Cemetery in the first place and went to the high school right next door, was quoted in the book as saying, "We often saw them on the street corner. They were there like it was the most normal thing in the world. I don't think the people who live nearby think ghosts are anything special at all."

Douryoudo Ato

Location: Yarimizu 401, Hachiouji City, Tokyo Metropolis, 192-0375

The local festival was over, but the two junior high students didn't want the fun to end there. The night was still young and there was even more fun to be had. It didn't take very long for them to agree upon their next stop; Douryoudo Ato, the supposedly haunted remains of an old temple from the Edo Period.

They climbed the long flight of stairs leading up to the temple and then entered the forest. They passed a stone that stated "Douryoudo" and then continued up even more stairs. The duo learnt about the so-called "Silk Road" that led to the temple when they were younger. Merchants used the path to sell their wares in Tokyo, and once upon a time, it was one of the busiest areas around. They even visited the temple remains on an elementary school trip.

But the atmosphere was completely different this time around. One of the boys looked at his friend, and he could tell immediately that he felt the same way. He was looking around, wide-eyed and nervous. The leaves rustled all around them as though coming to life. They were walking into the belly of the beast, and it was welcoming them with wide-open arms.

Even if he wanted to escape, the nearest area with light was further away than the temple remains were. The boy continued up the long flight of stairs, step by step, slowly approaching what felt like his doom. Finally, as his foot hit the last step, it hit him like a sack of bricks; they had arrived.

The temple remains were nothing but a base. It was near impossible to tell a temple ever once stood there. But the area was full of Jizo statues, and they were scattered and turned over. Fear rose within him once more. It wasn't right. They shouldn't be there.

"What's that?" his friend said suddenly, pointing to the middle of the remains. The boy looked over. There was indeed something there. His heart beat wildly. It appeared to be a tiny old woman, bending over to look at something. It was already past 8 p.m. and they were the only people around… other than the old woman, that was. Standing in the middle of the temple remains all by herself.

His friend couldn't hold it in any longer. He screamed and ran down the flight of stairs at full speed. The boy ran hot on his heels, and they ran until they reached the safety of the main road. They'd made it. They were safe. There was nothing to worry about anymore. The boys split up for the night and went their separate ways home.

A few days later, the boy's friend told him a story he heard from his father. He mentioned they went to Douryoudo Ato, and his father told him of an old woman who was murdered there long ago…

From the Edo Period until the beginning of the Meiji Period, there was a trade road connecting Yokohama to Kanagawa. Sellers sold their silk along it, and it came to be known as the Silk Road.

One stopover on the way was called Douryoudou, a temple. Now, nothing remains but the stone stairs, monuments, and the foundation stones of the temple. You can visit the remains in Otsukayama Park, located in Hachioji, to the west of Tokyo.

Rumours of ghosts first started appearing near the end of the Showa Period. In 1963, an old nun working at the temple was killed by a thief. Her body was found at 5:20 a.m. on the morning of September 10, 1963. The room she was discovered in was covered in blood, and there was evidence of knife-like wounds in her throat and chest. A zabuton cushion was placed over her face and the room was in disarray. Police believed the motive for the crime to be the money she kept on the premises, which was missing. After the nun was killed, the temple became abandoned with no-one to run it. In 1983, the abandoned temple was set on fire and burned to the ground, becoming the Douryoudou Ato (Douryoudou Remains).

10 years after the nun's murder, on September 6, 1973, a family of four was found drowned on a beach in Izucho, Shizuoka Prefecture. The family's personal items were found on a nearby rock wall, including a note indicating their suicide. The father of the family turned out to be a university professor, which sent the media into a frenzy. When the police investigated further, they discovered the horrific crime he had committed in life that led to his entire family's suicide.

It was discovered that the professor had killed one of his own students, who he had been having an affair with. He buried her body near his holiday house in Hachiouji, close to Douryoudou, and by the time her body was found, she had become mummified.

The holiday house was located a few kilometres away from Douryoudou, so strictly speaking, the incident had nothing to do with the area, but with the nun's death 10 years earlier, the media were looking for a story they could sell, so they connected the murders and a legend began. The holiday house itself is now a Christian church.

Ever since these two incidents, rumours of ghosts in the area have flourished, and it has become one of the most famous ghost spots in the West Tokyo area. People say you can hear the old nun's sobbing, and she often shows up in photos taken in the area as well. People have also mentioned they can hear footsteps that aren't their own when walking around the area. The university student's ghost appears quite frequently as well.

One of the stone statues on the grounds was also the basis for the famous ghost story "Kubinashi Jizo," (Headless Jizo) although the head has been repaired since then. It's said that the delinquents who originally trashed the statue arrived in a white car, so those who travel to the area in a white car will be cursed. Those who touch the statue may also be cursed. The area became so famous that to this day, groups of troublemakers make their way to the site in an attempt to vandalise the Jizo statue.

But that's not all. Douryoudou Ato is also famous for yet another urban legend, this time a yokai; Hitotsume Kozo, the one-eyed goblin. It's said that every year on December 8, the Hitotsume

Kozo appears to wreak havoc on the nearby villages. People hang bamboo baskets in front of their house to protect themselves from him. Records of this custom can be found in Hachiouji folklore and also in official records from the Silk Road.

Yamaguchi Bintarou, an occult researcher, went to Douryoudou Ato on December 8, 2014, to shed some more light on this Hitosume Kozo legend, but unfortunately never came across him. In fact, he discovered most people had never heard of the legend, and not one house hung a bamboo basket out the front. The only evidence he discovered was from an old man, born in the Taisho Period, who told him that when he was a child, his family used to hang a bamboo basket out the front of their house.

Douryoudou Ato is a site rich in history, but also rich in tragedy, making it an extremely popular ghost spot to this day.

Old Komine Tunnel

Location: Akikawa Highway, Kamikawa-machi, Hachiouji City, Tokyo Metropolis, 192-0151

The old friends were walking through the tunnel alone. But not just any tunnel. It was the Old Komine Tunnel. The scene of a horrific crime several decades earlier that shook Japan to its core. Now it was haunted, people said. You shouldn't go there. You never know what you might encounter.

But they were bored. They wanted to see what, if anything, was there. But his friend was a scaredy-cat, and as they walked through the gloomy tunnel, he gripped onto the back of his shirt like his life depended on it.

"Come on, man, let go," the young man told his friend. It was getting to be a bit much. They were both adults. He could walk through a dark and creepy tunnel without holding on to him. But he refused. He was too scared.

"Come on, I said let go."

It was starting to piss him off. He walked faster, hoping to shake his friend off that way. But he just gripped his shirt even harder, pulling on it.

"I said let go! Quit it!"

At boiling point, he turned around to give his friend a piece of his mind. But he wasn't there. He was standing roughly 10 metres away, the torch shaking in his hand.

There was no-one behind him.

When the pair got out of the tunnel, he noticed his friend's face was pure white. "What's wrong?"

he asked.

"I let go, like you asked." His voice trembled. "I was shining the flashlight in front of me as I walked, and then... I saw a woman... her hair was a mess. Then, from somewhere deep within the tunnel, I heard a strange voice... You didn't hear it?"

No, he didn't hear it. But he knew one thing. He didn't want to hang around that tunnel any longer...

Old Komine Tunnel sits on the old Akikawa Highway, now closed off to the public and running parallel to the New Komine Tunnel roughly 100 metres away. It's a small tunnel, built in 1912 and only 79.4 metres long, 4.3 metres wide and 3.5 metres high. It sits between Akiruno (formerly Itsukaichi) and Hachiouji cities. Combined with the narrow Akikawa Highway, where at least one section of the road is only wide enough for one car to pass at any time, it wasn't very safe, and thus a new, much larger tunnel and road were built.

The tunnel is famous these days for sightings of the ghost of a little girl, and the apparent ringing of a bell from somewhere inside the tunnel. While Komine Tunnel has long been known as a ghost spot, there was a very real tragedy that took place nearby that sealed its fate as one of the most famous ghost spots in Japan.

From 1988, the last year of the Showa Era, to 1989, the first year of the Heisei Era, four girls (aged four to seven-years-old) were murdered in the Tokyo and Saitama areas. These murders came to be known collectively as the "Tokyo/Saitama Serial

Little Girls Kidnapping and Murder Incident."

The murders shocked the nation, particularly when taking into account the girls' ages. Two of the girls were only four-years-old when murdered; the others, five and seven respectively. It wasn't just their ages, but also the brutality of their deaths that rocked Japan to its core. The man eventually arrested for their crimes was Miyazaki Tsutomu, a Tokyo native and a month shy of turning 27 at the time of his arrest.

Miyazaki was born in the suburb of Itsukaichi, located in the Nishitama district of Tokyo on August 21, 1962. His father was a prosperous man who ran a local newspaper, his grandfather was a member of the town council, and his great-grandfather had been a member of the village assembly, so the Miyazaki family were local celebrities.

Both his parents worked, so young Tsutomu was cared for by a male live-in nanny in his 30s who was said to be mentally disabled. The family lived with Miyazaki's grandparents, and his mother later gave birth to two girls, his younger sisters. Miyazaki was a shy, withdrawn child, but his grandfather doted on him, often taking him along on his walks.

Miyazaki was born with a rare disease which shaped much of his later life; congenital radioulnar synostosis. A rare disorder in which the radius and ulna fuse together at birth, meaning he was unable to turn his palms upwards. There were only 150 cases of the disease in all of Japan at the time.

The Miyazaki family visited the hospital to see if

anything could be done for the boy, but doctors informed them that "even if we perform surgery, there's only a one in one hundred chance that it will be successful." They recommended that if the young Tsutomu wasn't in pain, and if it wasn't affecting his daily life, then they should leave it be and wait until he got older.

And that's just what his parents did, but when Miyazaki started kindergarten, the other children started to pick on him because of his physical impairment. His teacher reportedly did nothing about the bullying, and times were tough for him.

When Miyazaki started elementary school, he was so into *kaiju*, or monsters, that the other kids called him Dr Kaiju. But this didn't mean that he was popular amongst his classmates. He did well at school, getting good grades in both math and English, although he struggled with Japanese and social studies.

In the first and second grades of junior high school he joined the athletics team, and then in the third grade he joined the shogi club. He took things extremely hard when he lost, and was known to read strategy books so he could best his opponents. Despite his physical disability, he learnt karate through a correspondence course, and was known to show off his moves to his classmates.

Miyazaki started going to the Meiji University-affiliated Nakano Junior and Senior High School in 1978, and it was around this time that he started to grow even more self-conscious of his physical impairment. It was a boys' school, and it took Miyazaki two hours one-way to get there each day.

His parents assumed he was travelling so far to such a prestigious school because he wanted to become an English teacher, but his classmates described him as a dark, gloomy student who didn't particularly stand out in any way. His grades started to fall, and while he wished to advance to Meiji University, his grades were so low that those hopes were quickly dashed.

In April 1981, Miyazaki started attending the Tokyo Polytechnic University, Junior College Department, in order to become a photo technician. He became obsessed with puzzles, submitting his own to specialised magazines and sending in his own answers to other published puzzles.

In 1982, he attended the NHK talk show *YOU* with a friend, but when the announcer approached him for an interview, Miyazaki hid behind the other guests. One of Miyazaki's classmates at the junior college, Kawasaki Mayo, later went on to become a famous actor, and at the time Miyazaki was arrested said, "I have a pretty good memory, and there were only 80 of us in the class so it's not like I'd forget him. But then, it was like, 'was he ever really there?' I asked our other classmates about him, but no-one remembers him." By this time, Miyazaki had withdrawn so much that people didn't even notice he was there.

Miyazaki graduated from junior college in 1983, and in April of the same year, his uncle recommended him to a print company in Kodaira City. He started working as a print operator, but his attitude towards the job was poor. His reputation among his coworkers was exceedingly bad. In

March 1986, a supervisor recommended that he move to another location in Kanagawa, but Miyazaki refused and instead quit. He locked himself in his room for the next few months, refusing his family's calls to help with the family business, but in September of the same year, he finally relented. He performed simple tasks, such as collecting advertising manuscripts for the newspaper.

Around this time, Miyazaki published a *doujinshi* (a fan comic of an existing anime or manga), but his actions caused the few friends he had to dislike him, and so he published no more. He then joined several video clubs, receiving and sharing recorded tapes from all around the country. But Miyazaki was content with simply collecting the tapes, and rarely watched them himself. He often made ludicrous and impossible requests to other video club members for dubbed videos, and in the end, they grew to dislike him as well. By the time of his arrest, Miyazaki had 5,763 video tapes in his collection.

On May 16, 1988, Miyazaki's beloved grandfather died. He fell even further into depression. Then, on August 22, the day after his 26th birthday, Miyazaki committed his first crime; he abducted and murdered a four-year-old girl named Konno Mari. He reportedly took the girl to Komine Ridge and sat with her for half an hour by the tunnel before finally murdering her. He then filmed himself performing perverse acts with her body and left her corpse in the Togura Hills, roughly two kilometres from Komine Tunnel.

Miyazaki later returned to cut off Konno's hands and feet, which he then kept in his closet. He then burnt the rest of her body, ground what was left into powder, and sent the ashes in a box to her parents on February 6, 1989, nearly six months after the girl had died. The box also included photos of her clothes and a postcard. The postcard said "Mari. Cremated. Bones. Investigate. Prove."

On October 3, 1988, Miyazaki abducted and murdered his second victim; seven-year-old Yoshizawa Masami. As with his first victim, Miyazaki first took the girl to the area near Komine Ridge where he then sexually molested her before killing her and abandoned her body in the Togura Hills.

Miyazaki abducted and killed four-year-old Namba Erika on December 9, 1988. He took her to a parking lot in Naguri, Saitama, and photographed her naked in the back of his car. He then killed her, tied her hands and feet behind her back, and put her in the trunk covered in a bed sheet.

But Namba had wet herself in his car while alive, and perhaps in his panic, Miyazaki hastily abandoned her body in the woods nearby. Her naked body was discovered on December 15, and a postcard arrived at her parents' house on December 20. The postcard said "Erika. Cold. Cough. Throat. Rest. Death." Namba's father appeared on TV and said that even though she was dead, he was glad they had found her body.

Miyazaki saw this and decided to deliver Yoshizawa's body to her parents as well. He went back to find it, but had trouble locating it. Witnesses reported seeing a "navy Nissan Langley," Miyazaki's car, on the mountain roads at the time.

During this time he also sent two letters to the Asahi Newspaper, pretending to be a woman and taking responsibility for the crimes. He confessed with fake details of the deaths; for instance, claiming that his first victim, Konno, drowned in the Iruma River. A handwriting specialist determined the letters to be from the same person, but because of the sharp angles of the handwriting, they were likely written using the person's non-dominant hand.

On June 6, 1989, Miyazaki abducted and killed his final victim; Nomoto Ayako, five-years-old. He claimed to police after his arrest that he cut off the girl's hands and ate them, but the prosecutor believed that he was embellishing his claims to appear more "abnormal." Nomoto's dismembered body was discovered in the hills five days after she was killed.

On July 23, 1989, Miyazaki was finally caught red-handed in Hachiouji, Tokyo. A girl caught him taking pictures of her naked sister and ran to inform their father. The father seized him until police arrived, unaware that he was the serial killer that had killed not only Nomoto a month before, but three other young girls over the previous year. Miyazaki confessed to Nomoto's murder on August 9, and then to Konno and Namba's murders on August 13. He finally confessed to Yoshizawa's murder on September 5, and her ashes were discovered in Itsukaichi the next day.

Miyazaki claimed that each time he killed one of

the girls he went home, placed a straw effigy in his room, put on a headband, lit several candles, put on dark clothes, and moved his hands up and down in a ritual aimed at bringing his grandfather back to life.

After his arrest, prosecutors claimed that his abnormal behaviour was thanks to the influence of his exceedingly large video tape collection, which included a healthy selection of anime, horror and porn films. He was called "The Otaku Murderer" and the media tried to blame these videos for making him commit such obscene acts.

74 investigators went through his entire collection over two weeks before they finally found his home movies of the crimes he'd committed, and while Miyazaki claimed he didn't know why he was compelled to kill the girls—or more bizarrely, that a "Rat Man" made him do it—Miyazaki was found guilty of the murders and sentenced to death on April 14, 1997. He was hung on June 17, 2008.

Not long after the murders of Konno and Yoshizawa, people claimed to see the ghost of a little girl near the tunnel. Even more witnesses claimed the ghost was missing its hands and feet, just like Konno. Was this just a coincidence, with people retroactively claiming to have seen the ghost after details of the girl's murder went public? Or had they really seen her, perhaps seeking help to bring her murderer to justice? Considering that rumours of the little girl ghost without hands or feet continue to this day, it would appear that, if true, Miyazaki's death wasn't enough to sate her spirit.

The New Komine Tunnel was finished in 2002, putting the old tunnel out of action. The old tunnel is now used as a walkway and has fallen into ruin, but it's also found new life somewhat as a popular *kimodameshi* spot.

Aoyama Cemetery

Location: Minami Aoyama 2 Chome 33, Minato Ward, Tokyo Metropolis, 107-0062

He was walking home around 2 a.m. after a long day at work. Long nights were nothing unusual, and as he passed by Aoyama Cemetery on his way home, he thought little of it. He passed by the cemetery all the time.

There were few people on the streets, but considering the time, that wasn't particularly strange either. But he didn't feel scared. He just wanted to get home and finally go to sleep. He picked up the pace. His comfortable bed was waiting for him.

A short distance past the cemetery he noticed something dark. In the dim streetlights it looked square, but it was moving. It was too small to be a person, but he was so tired that he wasn't terribly concerned about it either.

As he got closer and saw what it was, his heart stopped for a moment. It was an old lady in a wheelchair.

He didn't want to be rude and stare, so he did his best not to look at her. He walked past her, eyes focused on the ground, but then he heard a small voice. It sent a shiver down his spine.

"Help me."

He turned back to look at the old woman, his eyes widening in fear. Looking closer, he could tell immediately that the old woman was no longer of this world. Her eyes were nothing but large, gaping holes darker than the night itself...

Aoyama Cemetery is located in the south of Tokyo, close to Shibuya, and is a metropolitan cemetery. It opened in 1872 as a Shinto-only burial ground, but in 1874 it was opened to the public in general. It takes up about 260,000 square metres and houses over 100,000 gravesites. It's well known for being the final resting grounds of many famous people over the years.

You can find tombs for such figures as Okubo Toshimichi, a samurai of Satsuma and considered one of the founders of modern Japan; Komura Jutaro, a diplomat from the Meiji period; Nogi Maresuke, a general in the Imperial Japanese Army; several famous Kabuki actors who took the stage name of Ichikawa Danjuro over the years; and you can also find the tomb of the infamous Hachiko, the dog who waited in the same spot for his master to return day after day until he died. Hachiko's owner, Ueno Hidesaburo is also buried in Aoyama Cemetery, so Hachiko was buried next to him when he passed away nine years later.

But you won't just find graves in this cemetery; it's also one of the most famous ghost spots in Japan.

It's perhaps unavoidable for cemeteries to find themselves the subject of ghost stories, but Aoyama Cemetery in particular is especially famous for it. Although it's full of life during the day, the moment the sun sets and things get dark, the atmosphere changes completely. Perhaps due to its reputation as a ghost spot, it's rare to find people in or around the cemetery come nightfall. People new to the area often comment that they receive warnings not to hang around after dark, superstition or not, and many continue to heed that advice today.

You've probably heard of the urban legend where a taxi driver picks up a young woman from a cemetery late one night, but when he looks in the rear-view mirror a short while later, the woman is gone. Not only is she gone, but the back seat is also completely drenched. There are other versions where the cemetery is the destination rather than the pickup, but in either case, the original cemetery in this legend is Aoyama.

There are rumours that many taxis refuse to pick passengers up from Aoyama Cemetery at night, even today, and very few pass by in the first place. It's not just taxis, either. Bus drivers have reported the "STOP" light inside their buses going off as they approach the stop near Aoyama Cemetery even though no-one is on-board.

Another famous story tells of a group of youths who visited the cemetery late at night for a test of courage, but were then dragged into another world. There are supposedly several locations around the cemetery that link to a different world, but no-one knows for sure where they are. If you're going to the cemetery at night, be careful. You might not return.

Other visitors to the cemetery have remarked seeing signs with "!" on them. In general, a sign with "!" on it is usually followed by a set of rules or warnings that people need to heed, such as "Don't walk on the grass" or "Be careful of traffic." Yet this particular sign has no warnings, simply a large "!" on it. So what does it mean?

If you see one of these signs, chances are it's warning you that there are ghosts about. The signs pop up all over the park, and according to the rumours, when they do, you best get out of there quick-smart. Ghosts are on the prowl, and you don't want to be around for them to find you.

But that's still not all for one of the most haunted cemeteries in Japan. There are also stories of two shadows that can be seen floating in the area during the night. What they do exactly depends on the people who witness them; some have claimed they get sucked into thin air, while others have seen them appear suddenly out of nowhere whilst driving. The two shadows are different sizes, one small, one large, leading many to believe they are the shadows of a mother and child not quite laid to rest yet. They've been known to cause accidents by appearing suddenly in front of cars and haunting people within the park.

If you ever find your way to Aoyama Cemetery, particularly during spring, it's a popular area to walk around due to the beautiful cherry blossoms. Just be mindful of the time. You really don't want to get caught there at night. No need to add yet another story to the already long list.

Kohoku Bridge

Location: 2 Chome, Ogi, Adachi Ward, Tokyo Metropolis, 123-0873

Several years ago, a young man crossed over the Kohoku Bridge in Adachi Ward to get to work every day. The bridge was infamous for the large number of accidents that took place there. People often crashed into the guardrails, or even into the river, claiming the bridge curved when, in reality, it was straight as a rod. Lights were installed on the guardrails to keep people from driving into them, and slowly the number of accidents decreased.

On this particular day, the young man faced problem after problem at work, and it wasn't until 10 p.m. that night that he finally approached the bridge on his way home. He was almost there. He would finally be able to relax and put the day behind him. But suddenly the handle of his scooter turned of its own accord. He lost balance and crashed.

Other than some scrapes and bruises he was okay, but the incident shook him. It was like something fell onto his handlebars, making them turn wildly and causing the scooter to crash. He was sober, clear-headed, and had a perfect view of what was in front of him, so what happened?

He chalked it up to a freak accident and left the scene. He knew of the ghostly rumours surrounding the bridge, but was it just a coincidence that his scooter turned all by itself, or was there some truth to the rumours of spirits attempting to drag people to join them in the depths below…?

Located in Adachi, north of Shinjuku, the Kohoku Bridge is known as one of the most haunted spots in Tokyo. The bridge is well-known for repeated traffic accidents, and over the years many ghost sightings followed, giving it a reputation as one of the most haunted bridges in the capital.

It all started about 30 years ago. On December 12, 1989, a car broke through the guardrail and drove over the edge of the bridge into the river. The driver was never found. After this, several cars drove over the edge of the bridge in repeated accidents. According to reports, the drivers claimed that while they were driving, their vision warped and the bridge seemed to curve to one side. As they turned the steering wheel to follow this abrupt curve of the bridge, they drove over the edge. As a result of this, the bridge was remodelled in the mid-90s and the guardrails were strengthened, causing a drop in the number of accidents.

In addition to these accidents, drivers and pedestrians walking over the bridge claim to have seen a female ghost floating nearby. This female ghost is perhaps the most commonly seen at the bridge, although it's unknown whether she was the victim of an accident there or lived in the area in the first place. Others have reported being chased by a man on a bike, and other such variety of ghosts.

Such a large number of accidents have occurred at the bridge over the years that rituals have been held to purify the area, but they've had no effect. A famous medium went to the bridge in order to purify it, but was quoted as saying, "Nothing can be done here." People also claim that if you walk across the bridge at night, you'll be cursed.

Not only single ghosts, but groups of ghosts are said to hang out underneath the bridge. People playing baseball on the field near the riverbed, or those just walking by may be unlucky enough to run into them. One man who went to watch a game of baseball reported that he felt a distinct tap on his shoulder, but when he turned around no-one was there. A medium who visited the area felt that this was because the geography under the bridge acted as a type of "ghost magnet." The undulation of the river helps to strengthen that, and as the bridge was built over the top of it, it made it prone to accidents and ghostly appearances.

Other incidents that people have reported happening at the bridge are as follows:

1. The sound of drums and accompanying orchestra luring people over the edge of the bridge.
2. When driving over the bridge, drivers suddenly find themselves tired and without enough energy to even grip the steering wheel. When they turn to look out the driver's side window, they can see a pale-faced woman staring at them.
3. An elderly spirit and his dog can be seen walking along the footpath.
4. People trying to take photos from the top of the bridge can find their shutter refuses to work, even though it works perfectly fine

when pointed at something else.

Whether any of these ghostly sightings are actually true or not, the fact remains that the bridge is a hotspot for accidents, so if you ever go there, make sure to be very careful when crossing over..

Shakujii Park

Location: Shakujiidai, Nerima Ward, Tokyo Metropolis, 177-0045

A group of six friends were travelling around Tokyo visiting various ghost spots. The final stop on their tour was Shakujii Park, a rather large and beautiful park in Nerima Ward. They heard about a mound that was supposed to be haunted, but after searching for it for close to 20 minutes, they were unable to find it.

The group decided to go home. It was getting late, and they'd seen enough for one night anyway. One young man hung behind with his friend as the other four walked ahead of them. Everyone was chatting and joking, and the atmosphere was cheerful. But as they were passing the pond, the young man heard a sound from the water. It sounded like something breaking the surface.

He looked fearfully at his friend and they turned around. Nothing was there. Perhaps they were just hearing things. He turned back and continued talking to his friend. This time he heard footsteps on the gravel behind them. His friend heard it too. This time they didn't turn around. They took off running as fast as their feet would carry them.

"Run!" they screamed as they ran past their four friends. It wasn't until they reached the exit that they stopped to turn around. Nobody was there, but just for a moment, the young man saw what looked like the figure of a person disappearing back into the lake.

One of his friend's later told him that there used to be a castle on the park grounds, and the owner of that castle committed suicide in the lake. Did that mean the figure he saw was…?

Shakujii Park is located in the west of Tokyo and is one of the largest parks in the city. It houses two ponds, several small Shinto shrines and the remains of Shakujii Castle. If you believe the rumours, it's also home to several ghosts.

Shakujii Castle was ruled by the Toshima clan in the 1400s. In 1477, the then-leader Toshima Yasutsune fought against the armies of Ota Dokan in the Kyotoku Rebellion. Toshima lost, however, and retreated to his castle as the Ota armies advanced. Seeing that his time was near, it's said Toshima grabbed his family treasure, the Golden Saddle, and fled from the back of the castle on his white horse. The Ota soldiers watched him as both Toshima and the horse went over a cliff and into the Sanpoji Pond.

Toshima's daughter, the beautiful Teruhime, was so sad at her father's death that she followed him into the pond and drowned as well. Ota felt pity for her and held a memorial service for her death, building a burial mound that came to be known as *Himetsuka* (princess mound), which you can still visit in the park today. It was said back in the day that if you climbed the old pine tree by the side of the mound, you could see both Toshima and his Golden Saddle radiating brilliantly at the bottom of the pond. A festival is now held in the area each year called Teruhime Matsuri, which includes processions around the park and stage plays of the above story.

But that isn't where the story ends. In modern times, people claim that you can see the face of a woman floating in the pond, perhaps Teruhime herself. If you stare into the surface of the water, before long you'll find a woman's face staring back at you. In addition, if you point your camera towards the pond to take a picture, it's said that a woman will appear in the photo, not quite human, not quite mist, but something in-between.

But that's still not all. Legend goes that ever since the Edo period, lovers who meet by the lake will meet a disastrous end. A beautiful woman on a white horse (sound familiar?) appears out of the water, beckoning the man to her. Unable to resist her lure, the man follows her into the water, disappearing forever. The next day the woman finds herself drawn to the pond, and can be heard muttering, "The Golden Saddle calls. There's a castle in the pond," before she too disappears, never to be seen again.

Rumours then spread in the 1980s that a police officer was killed by the pond, and that a crazy old man jumped into the pond in the middle of winter and drowned, just like Toshima and Teruhime before him. The area has since become a famous hotspot for ghost sightings and even people looking for the lost treasure of the Toshima clan. Residents of the area also claim that if you walk around the pond at night, you can feel a presence following you.

As an aside and entirely unrelated to the story of

Toshima and his daughter Teruhime, in 1993, there were eyewitness reports of a giant crocodile in the Sanpoji Pond. Quite a bit of fuss was kicked up, but in the end, the giant crocodile was never found. Maybe it was looking for the Toshima family gold as well.

Sunshine 60

Location: 3-1-1 East Ikebukuro, Toshima Ward, Tokyo Metropolis, 170-6090

He was the manager of the haunted house in the basement of Sunshine 60, the former tallest building in Tokyo. Buddhist prayers played as background music all day long, and during quiet times, he found himself drifting off to sleep while listening to them.

Bang!

Something hit the wall of the manager's room. He looked around, but he was the only one there. He chalked it up to a figment of his imagination, but when he told one of his employees about it later, they revealed they had all heard the same sound at least once, always when no-one was around. A chill ran down his spine… But that wasn't the end of it.

There was a room, partitioned with a curtain, that kept the switch to operate the monsters inside the haunted house. Employees could see when customers were passing by and press the button to move the machines at the right time. The room had no solid roof, but every now and then when an employee looked up, they complained they could see the face of a small child looking down at them…

Sunshine 60 in Ikebukuro was built in 1978, and at the time of its completion was the tallest building in Asia. Reaching 239.7 metres, it has 60 floors, just like its name, but depending on who you listen to, there's another reason the skyscraper has the number "60" attached.

The land Sunshine 60 now stands on used to be Sugamo Prison. Operating from 1895 to 1971, the prison famously held political prisoners and later suspected war criminals after the end of World War II. Inside the prison was a metal door with the number "13" painted on it. This was the door that led 60 prisoners to their deaths, including seven A class war criminals. People claimed that even within the room there were 13 steps leading to the hangman's noose, the preferred method of execution.

60 executions. 60 floors. Sunshine 60. A coincidence, or something more?

There are several rumours regarding the mysterious happenings in Sunshine 60. One legend stated that there was a single floor of the building that was so dangerous, a security guard was placed there to keep people out. More rumours claimed it to be the 42nd floor, but this was quickly debunked. The 42nd floor is a business office with regular employees coming and going all the time. There's no security guard keeping people out because of angry spirits. People theorised this rumour came about because in Japanese 42 could be split into "four = shi" and "two = ni," with *shini* meaning death.

Another legend states that the original 13 steps of the death chamber still exist inside the basement of the building. If you manage to find and climb those stairs, you will be cursed and within two weeks suffer a terrible injury or even die.

But why would workers destroy a prison and

leave only 13 steps behind? Because, according to rumour, any workers who tried to knock them down suffered great misfortune, and so in the end it was decided to leave them be and simply build the new building over them, hiding them deep in the bowels. People have searched for the stairs for years and never found them. Probably because a quick glance at this legend should set off alarm bells of suspicion, but who doesn't love a good story? There is, however, a fourth level in the basement that is off-limits to the public, so who knows? Perhaps there is something hidden down there after all?

Another popular legend regarding the skyscraper says that not long after construction was completed, someone jumped from the top floor. Their spirit, along with many others, continues to haunt the building to this day, and it's not uncommon to see floating orbs or capture unexplainable things when taking photos in the area.

Even wilder legends tell of the spirit of an old woman who can reach up to 80 km/h. They call her "Mach Obasan," or Mach Old Lady. You must be careful not to let her catch you, because it won't end well if she does. But considering she can run at speeds of 80 km/h, you probably don't have much of a chance once she's got her sights set on you. She's joined in the area by the Headless Rider, the spirit of a man who supposedly lost his head in a motorcycle accident nearby.

The next time you're heading to Ikebukuro for a spot of shopping and sightseeing, beware. You might get a little more than you originally bargained for… or so ghost hunters would have you believe.

Nijinoo Bridge

Location: Prefectural Road 64, Miyagase, Kiyokawa Village, Aiko District, Kanagawa Prefecture, 243-0111

It was midday, and the young man was approaching Nijinoo Bridge on his bike. He noticed a woman in a white dress standing on the walkway. This was nothing strange or new. The bridge was a popular throughway and the view from the top was beautiful. One of the best sites in Kanagawa.

There was a single car in front of him as they neared the middle of the bridge. The woman turned and all of a sudden threw herself in front of the car. The driver didn't even have time to think. He slammed his brakes on and slid across the bridge. The young man followed suit, nearly slamming into the car at full speed and only just narrowly avoiding a collision.

The driver got out of the car, the blood draining from his face.

"You saw that, right? She… she jumped, right? You saw that, right?"

The man was white and trembling all over, tears forming in his eyes. The two men walked around to the front of the car. There was nobody there…

Nijinoo Bridge, known in Japanese as *Niji no Oohashi* (Rainbow Bridge) is an arch bridge that can be found on Prefectural Road 64 in Kanagawa crossing over Miyagase Lake. It was selected as one of the top 100 bridges in Kanagawa in 1991 by a public vote, coming in at 87th. It sits on the border of Midori Ward in Sagamihara City and Kiyokawa Village. It goes by the English nickname of "Rainbow Bridge" to many of the locals.

The bridge was constructed in 1985. The arch section of the bridge is 210 metres long, while the entire length from start to finish measures 330 metres. When the bridge was first built, it ran over the Hayato River at a rather high elevation, close to 150 metres from the bridge to the river below. However, in 2000, the nearby Miyagase Dam was finished, creating Miyagase Lake and flooding the area with water. The distance from the bridge to the water below dramatically decreased. Combined with the beauty of the nearby scenery, tourists visit Nijinoo Bridge all year around.

Due to the height of the bridge when it was first constructed, it became a popular choice for people looking to commit suicide. Several people threw themselves from the bridge into the depths below, and eventually the problem became so persistent that a large two-metre fence was erected on both sides to deter people from climbing over it. But by that point the bridge also had a reputation as a popular suicide spot, so people continued to climb over the fence regardless.

As you would expect, a lot of rumours started to spread about the bridge. People claimed that the white shadow of a woman would float in the air on the other side of the fence, glaring at people on it. Others claimed that if you took a picture of the lake below from the bridge, chances would be high that you'd capture a spirit or floating orb in the developed photo. Other rumours stated that, if you stood on the edge of the bridge, suddenly you would hear footsteps come running towards you out of nowhere. Yet another rumour said that something would grab and pull your hair from behind whilst driving over the bridge.

A common feature you'll find with most Japanese ghosts is their connection to water. This has been so for hundreds of years. Water connects our physical world to their spiritual world. It is through water that the spirit crosses over, in both directions. There is a long-held superstition that people must not swim during Obon, the festival during which spirits return to the world of the living to visit their families, because if you do, you may get swept up with the spirits and spirited away yourself. This makes bridges popular ghost spots, because it's said the undulation of the waves beneath the man-made structures amplifies a spirit's powers. Nijinoo Bridge is, of course, no different.

Like the sediment of the river below, the grudges of those who have died at the bridge is said to build and continue accumulating as long as the spirits are unable to move on. One medium who visited the area claimed that before the Miyagase Dam was built, the area had a good spiritual flow, but after the water was blocked up, that quickly turned negative, and now the spirits are unable to leave.

These days there's a sign on the bridge that says:

If you discover   around Miyagase Dam,
   if you discover something strange,
Please alert the following.

It's unknown whether the white spaces have always been there, have faded away with time, or have been deliberately erased by people who are messing around, but it helps lend to the eerie air of this well-known suicide spot. If it was placed there to stop people from ending their lives on the bridge, it certainly hasn't helped.

On February 13, 2017, witnesses saw an ambulance, three fire trucks, a rescue car, and a police command car on the bridge with two boats searching the river below around 3 p.m. that day. A bag full of female personal items was discovered on the bridge. It's unknown whether the body was recovered.

On August 23, 2018, news started to spread throughout Twitter that a mass suicide had taken place at Nijinoo Bridge. Police cars and fire trucks swarmed the area, and passersby noticed several cars stopped on the bridge, but no sign of any drivers or passengers. Boats were also seen searching the area below the bridge, leading many to suspect that it was indeed another suicide.

While the incident didn't make nationwide news, it was reported across several websites in real-time. According to eyewitnesses, three people were seen walking along the bridge, although whether they were related to the incident was unknown. A single shoe was found on the bridge along with some personal effects, and while it was initially thought to be a mass suicide, it turned out to be a single man in his twenties.

Like other famous suicide spots around the country, it seems unlikely people will stop visiting

Nijinoo Bridge to end their lives any time soon. Its reputation as one of the most popular ghost spots around Japan seems likely to live on for quite some time to come.

CHUBU

Niigata Russia Village

Location: 1956 Sasaoka, Agano City, Niigata Prefecture, 959-1918

They were there for work. Two comedians prepared to entertain and amuse for a "ghosts captured on film" special planned for that summer. The location? The infamous Niigata Russia Village. An abandoned theme park that was the site of numerous ghost photos over the years. It was the perfect location. Dark. Abandoned. Creepy. It was even featured on another special the year before where some entertainers managed to capture some ghosts on film. What could go wrong?

The basement of the Maly Hotel was said to be the most haunted spot. Previously the site of an arson attempt, very little was left of the original building, but a broken boiler in the basement left constantly dripping over the years had flooded the area, making it cold, dirty and wet. The perfect location to capture something otherworldly on film.

Before they even entered the building, the female comedian felt someone—or something—looking at her. She could see nothing, but she could feel its gaze upon her. Photos of ghostly orbs in the building were especially common. Was one of the spirits watching her?

The moment they stepped inside, she stopped. She could hear a voice. Something inside the building was trying to speak to her. It wasn't until a priest later viewed the tape that they discovered what the voice was trying to tell her.

"Hurry up and get out!"

The comedians made their way down into the basement. Water sat 50cm high, and other than the light from their cameras, it was pitch black. In the corner of the room they managed to capture something that looked like a face, but in the dark it was hard to tell.

Then, suddenly, the male comedian started crying. The sadness of the ghosts who were forced to linger in the dark, wet conditions was too much to bear. They took control of him, just briefly, to express how they felt. Or so it was thought…

Opened on September 1, 1993, as a way to spread Russian culture to the Japanese, Niigata Russia Park takes up an area of 40,000 square metres in the north of Niigata Prefecture. The park was a first for Niigata, and a hot topic of conversation when it finally opened. But visitors were few, and financing the park became more and more difficult. In the end, the difficult decision was made to close it, and its final day open to the public was in April 2004, less than 10 years after it first opened.

The park was left as-is when it closed. The buildings, the display goods, even the furnishings were left intact. This, and the fact that the park was in the middle of nowhere, attracted a great many trespassers. It wasn't long until the park was a mess, like something out of an apocalyptic movie, and over time, weather destroyed what people didn't.

In 2009, somebody lit a fire in the Maly Hotel section of the park. This led to recommendations to finally destroy and remove the rest of the buildings, and in 2014, they started demolitions. Only the church and hotel buildings remain, and they are still popular sites for trespassers, ghost hunters, and entertainers looking to cash in on some chilling summer TV.

In a TV special for the program *Sekai no Kowai Yoru!* (Scary World Nights), comedic group Panther and entertainer Imai Hana visited the park to try to capture some ghosts on film. They entered the basement of the Maly Hotel, alone and in groups, trying to capture something supernatural for the world to see.

Shortly after entering the building, Ogata, one of the Panther members, was overcome with a migraine. Nervous and unwell, he proceeded into the basement with the other members. He captured what sounded like voices in the water, and disturbing handprints on the walls. Ogata later went in again by himself and captured a dark shadow falling into the water. He fled the scene in the panic, and a medium waiting outside claimed that it was a spirit complaining about his presence. The spirit was angry that he was there. Its anger at being trapped in such conditions over the years was causing its rage to manifest physically. One misstep and he would have been in serious mortal danger.

Imai then went to film the bathroom alone, and unknown to even herself at the time, captured what looked like a ghost in the toilet stall as she fled. She found black markings like soot on her hand when she got outside. She claimed she never touched anything inside the building, nor did she see the spirit she captured on film. Did she simply rub up against a burnt wall on her way out, or was it something more sinister?

Niigata Russia Village is also famous for doors that open and close by themselves, a woman's screams in the dead of night, and the strange deaths of those who become possessed by the angry spirits they take home by mistake. By why is it haunted? Niigata Russia Village never had any accidents while it was in operation. There were no deaths, no murders, and nothing that might make it the breeding ground for angry spirits. So why?

Rumours started after the park closed that a woman entered the hotel basement and drowned in the water. You can still see her ghost down there even now, angry and unable to move on. Is it her scream that haunts the park to this day?

Word then passed around the local area that the park was a good spot for people to commit suicide. It was large, empty, and full of dangerous traps and potholes. If someone was looking to end their life, the park may have seemed like an attractive choice.

Either way, rumours grew and spread outside of Niigata and into Japan at large. The most common and prominent remains that of the Maly Hotel basement. No matter who you talk to, that basement is dangerous, and you shouldn't go inside.

Tsubono Well

Location: Prefectural Road 67, Tsubono, Uozu City, Toyama Prefecture, 937-0827

A group of four students were bored and decided to visit Tsubono Well, the infamous "Spiriting Away Hotel." Two young women visited the hotel for *kimodameshi* in the past and were never seen again, leading people to believe they were spirited away upon visiting the building.

The area was a famous hot spring, and the building was once a prosperous ryokan. But there were rumours that the hotel owner killed himself, and shortly thereafter, the building was left abandoned.

The group was just looking for a bit of fun, so they jumped in the car and drove over. The building sat in the middle of nowhere, the perfect spot for a little fun away from prying eyes. It was the middle of summer, but when they arrived, they felt a chill. It was cold enough for a jacket.

The front door was locked, so they climbed through a nearby open window, one by one. They used their phones to light the way, barely able to see each other's faces in the gloom. The roof above their heads was rotten and caving in; they were more worried about that coming down and killing them all than any ghosts that might be around.

But even so, it was a famous ghost spot, and they really wanted to see something spooky. They discovered some stairs, and proceeded to the second floor, hoping to find something a little more fruitful up there. The stairs were covered in dust from years of disuse. They then went through each room, looking for something, anything, that might be of interest. They found empty concrete bathrooms and damp tatami mats, but very little else.

"Hello! Is anyone there!" one of the boys yelled out. They joked around, tossing things and playing in the empty rooms. But then suddenly…

Splash.

They heard the sound of someone stepping in a puddle. It was sunny outside, and they hadn't seen any water on their way through the building.

They looked at each other. The hairs on their arms stood on end. Either way, they were no longer alone. The group took off running towards the stairs, their footsteps thundering throughout the building as they rushed for the window, unable to turn back and see what might be waiting for them…

The Tsubono Well ryokan went bankrupt in 1982, leaving behind an eight-story building on 3,300 square metres of land in the middle of Uozu City, Toyama Prefecture. According to some rumours, the owner vanished without a trace. Others claimed he committed suicide. Either way, the building was left abandoned, standing tall in the mountains of Tsubono.

The hot springs on the hotel grounds were salty, and said to be effective for people suffering from skin diseases, nerve pain, gastrointestinal disorder, and women's diseases. They brought people from all around the country to visit their healing waters. But the hotel was still burning money, and so the owners were forced to close it, leaving the building behind. The hot springs are still there, of course, but after being abandoned for close to forty years now, the accommodations aren't quite as nice as they used to be.

At 9 p.m. on May 5, 1996, two 19-year-old girls from Himi City told their parents, "We're going out for *kimodameshi*," got in the car, and were never seen again. The girls' destination was Tsubono Well; the police were able to determine this from a message the girls paged their friends: "We're in Uozu City now." The girls were also seen on National Highway 8, heading towards Uozu City, around 10 p.m. that night.

The two girls were high school friends. At the time of their disappearance, one girl was a company employee, and the other (the owner of the car) worked at a supermarket. Yet, what happened to them that night remains unknown. A large-scale search was conducted, but they found no sign of the girls; even the car was gone. It wasn't until March 1997, a year later and when the girls would have been 20 (making them legal adults) that the police went to the public looking for information on their whereabouts. To this date, nothing has ever been found of the pair.

So what happened to them? As is common for abandoned buildings, violent gangs took up residence in Tsubono Well not long after it was abandoned. It became a famous ghost spot for its creepy nature, but it also became a popular hangout for teenagers and young adults looking for a place to get away from it all and run wild. But did yakuza and bike gangs have anything to do with the girls' disappearances, or was it something else entirely?

There are various supernatural legends surrounding Tsubono Well. Supposedly, the owner hung himself and his spirit haunts the building to this day. Others claim you can see the spirit of a child who drowned in the pool. The boiler room is also haunted. There are ghosts all over the building, and if the yakuza don't get you, they will. There are even a list of conditions you must meet if you wish to return from Tsubono Well safely:

1. You must not drive to the building in your own car.
2. You mustn't drive to the building in a white car.
3. You must take care when opening doors.
4. You mustn't go alone.
5. You mustn't say your name or give out any other personal information when inside the building.
6. You must visit a temple or shrine to be purified after visiting the building.

If you fail to meet these conditions, there can be no guarantee for your safety… if you believe the rumours, that is.

Gibo Aiko, the famous spirit medium who seems to appear in every ghost spot story, reportedly visited the hotel for a TV program and proclaimed how dangerous the place was. But whether you believe the stories or not, the fact remains that the building itself is dangerous and on the verge of falling apart after forty years left untouched. It's not a safe place to visit for any reason.

White House

Location: 1 Wakasugi-cho, Fukui City, Fukui Prefecture, 918-8055

In a house located in Fukui City, there was once an incident so terrible that the house was left abandoned forever. An incident so horrific that it couldn't be contained to the lot it took place on and instead spread, infecting the neighbours.

At first glance, there was nothing special about the house. It was a plain house that you might see anywhere, but thanks to its white walls, people came to call it the "White House." A family lived inside that house, and they were happy. For a period, anyway.

The father slowly started to go mad. Nobody knew why, but day by day his neurosis grew, until finally something overcame him. He couldn't hold it in any longer, and on that night, the father killed his entire family before taking his own life.

But the madness didn't end there. Whatever infected the father spread, and according to the local newspaper, the family next door soon experienced the same madness, followed by the massacre of their entire family...

Rumours about a small two-story house in Fukui City started to spread around 2006. Located smack bang in the middle of a residential area, the building was perpetually empty, and word on the street was that a father killed his entire family inside. Ever since that horrific incident, the real estate was unable to get anyone else to live there and so the building deteriorated, eventually becoming uninhabitable.

Nobody knew who this supposed father and his family were, but as the rumours spread, word got out that the neighbours of the so-called White House were affected by the same madness, and the father of that household also killed his family. It was a double family suicide.

People claimed that they could see a woman looking down at them from the second-floor window with bloodshot eyes. Perhaps glaring, or perhaps pleading. Her voice and footsteps could be heard when no-one was around, indicating some awful event that had once taken place on that very floor. But if this were true, if two families were really involved in a murder-suicide, wouldn't more people know about it?

One man went to Fukui City to investigate the truth behind the rumours, using information gathered from residential maps in the local library and information from the city hall. He discovered that no-one ever lived in the house. It was empty all along, and was most likely just a residential office that was never used. There were never any family murder-suicides either; the person who lived on one side of the house lived alone, and the other neighbours are still living in the same house today, alive and well.

Where did the rumours come from? There are several "White Houses" around Japan. There's another in Niigata Prefecture, one in Chiba, one in Ibaraki, and one in Hokkaido as well. These White

Houses all have the same story with slightly different details, but they all end in a family being murdered, and almost all involve the event happening on the second floor. It is from this creepy, abandoned second floor that the ghost of each particular White House looks down upon the street, hoping for someone to free them from their confinement.

The Fukui City White House was finally knocked down in 2016 after years of deterioration, and the lot remains empty at present.

Futamata Tunnel

Location: National Highway 418, Minato, Yaotsu-cho, Kamo District, Gifu Prefecture, 505-0532

People called it the "Korean Tunnel," although that wasn't its official name. There were rumours that Korean workers were used to build it, and that they were literally worked to death inside its walls.

The tunnel had long been closed, but it was still accessible by foot. There was a large cliff nearby, and it wasn't unusual to see bouquets of flowers lining the path in commemoration of those who had taken their lives there. The number of suicides was supposedly rising in recent years.

But he still wanted to see it. They had come this far after all. The tunnel was just ahead. The infamous Futamata Tunnel, one of the most haunted locations in Gifu. Some even said that the first sightings of Kuchisake-onna were at that very tunnel. It was their claim to fame. Any teenager worth their salt had to go and see it firsthand.

There were flowers outside the tunnel. The young man hesitated before stepping inside with his friend. Rumours said that you could hear the screams of a woman inside, or that shadows would appear to chase you out. But he just felt sick. There were no ghosts. No screams. Nothing but an overwhelming urge to throw up. He couldn't be there any longer. He told his friend, who was disappointed, but agreed they should go home.

When they got back, they saw something that froze the blood in their veins. Handprints, all over the car. So many that they couldn't count them all. They were small, like that of a child.

A joke. It was just some other kids playing a prank. That was all.

A few days later, his friend had an accident. He was okay, but his car was destroyed. The pair later found out that the wife of a Korean worker went to visit the tunnel when he never came home. She also went missing and was never seen again. She was pregnant at the time…

The Futamata Tunnel finished construction in May 1956. It runs alongside the Kiso River in Gifu Prefecture on National Highway 418 and is just shy of 400 metres in length. The roads leading into Futamata Tunnel are now closed, and the only way to access it is on foot. This is fairly easy to do, but there are numerous sheer cliffs along the way.

There were plans for the tunnel to become submerged once the New Maruyama Dam finished construction nearby, but due to difficulties, those plans were abandoned and the tunnel still stands freely beside the river today.

The origins behind the name "Futamata" are unknown. The word *futamata* refers to something being split in two. Some have suggested it's because the tunnel was originally split in two, with part of the tunnel leading towards the river where people offloaded goods. There's no evidence that this was ever the case, however, and it's possible that the name was adopted simply as a place name.

These days it's more well known as the "Korean Tunnel." Rumours have long persisted that Korean labourers were used to build the tunnel, and that many of them were literally worked to death. They were pushed from morning till night with very little food, and if someone died on the job, their body was buried inside the tunnel walls as a *hitobashira*, or human pillar. There is no proof of this ever having taken place, but the rumours persist to this day and the name has stuck.

The tunnel itself is rather unique. It doesn't run in a straight line, but rather twists and turns, and the height and width are constantly uneven. There are no lights inside the nearly 400-metre long tunnel, so if you don't bring one with you, it's impossible to see anything inside. And as you might expect from such a creepy, abandoned tunnel, it comes with a swathe of ghost stories on the side as well.

The most common story is that of the Korean labourers being worked to death and then buried inside the tunnel walls. Their angry spirits are said to stalk the tunnel until this day, and if you enter the tunnel alone, beware. There have been stories of people being surrounded by shadows, and their shoulders suddenly becoming heavy, making it difficult to stand up straight. If you're especially unlucky, the shadows will chase you out of the tunnel completely, but it doesn't end there. It's not uncommon for people who travel to the tunnel by car to be involved in an accident days or even weeks after visiting the area. If they don't get you inside the tunnel, the spirits have no problem following you back and causing you grief at a later date.

Another famous rumour is that someone once

saw a woman near the tunnel with her mouth torn wide open. This woman was, of course, Kuchisake-onna, and stories of her soon spread nationwide. Gifu Prefecture does lay claim to the origins of the Kuchisake-onna legend, so it's not too much of a stretch to see why people would try to connect the two. A haunted tunnel, a creepy woman who likes to kill… it's a match made in heaven. Or perhaps hell.

If you hang around the tunnel at night, chances are good that you'll hear the screams of a solitary woman inside its walls. Who is she? Nobody knows for sure, but no haunted place is complete without an angry female ghost. Perhaps she was killed by the ghosts inside the tunnel herself. Or perhaps the stories of Korean labourers being buried inside the walls of the tunnel weren't scary enough and ghost hunters needed a little extra incentive to visit. Just like we expect to get a phone call if we watched a cursed tape, people expect to find a female ghost at a haunted location. There doesn't need to be a reason why. There just needs to be one.

There's no evidence that Korean labourers ever worked on the tunnel, nor that Kuchisake-onna's first "official" sighting was nearby. But when have we ever let the truth stand in the way of a good ghost story?

Shimoda Fujiya Hotel

Location: 3 Kakisaki, Shimoda, Shizuoka Prefecture, 415-0013

They were there to film a summer special. TV shows about ghosts were all the rage, and they had something special lined up. They were sending some popular comedians to film inside an abandoned hotel by the seaside. The story practically wrote itself.

The Shimoda Fujiya Hotel. Once popular with tourists in the 60s and 70s, but abandoned after the economic bubble burst. It's unique design and leftover furniture from decades past made it the perfect location to film. But then something happened that they weren't expecting.

They noticed a change in one of the female staff members. She was doubled over, seemingly in pain and acting strangely. The spirit medium that was accompanying the filming rushed over. It didn't take him long to figure out what was wrong.

"She's been possessed. There's two of them."

The staff member looked up at him and suddenly started laughing. It was no ordinary laugh. It wasn't coming from her, but rather, the spirits inside her…

Shimoda Fujiya Hotel can be found on Higashi-Izu Road in the seaside town of Shimoda in Shizuoka prefecture. Overlooking the water, this hotel is just one of several in the area, and although it is now permanently closed, the abandoned ruins remain. It is also commonly known simply as F Hotel.

The hotel is located in the area where Matthew Perry forced the ports of Shimoda open to American trade in 1854, and was also the location of the first American Consulate in Japan, which was opened just down the road by Consul General Townsend Harris. A memorial stone to Perry and the temple used as the first American Consulate can both be found today just a few hundred metres away from the remains of the hotel.

The hotel was in business during the 1960s and 70s, but has now been abandoned for over 30 years. With its complex design, the building was unique for its time, and the rooms inside were designed with a mature, traditional Japanese feel. Viewed from the outside, the hotel appears to be several unrelated buildings slapped together. There are several uneven levels, parts of the building are curved, and in total, it's spread out over a rather wide area with pieces of the building jutting in and out with no apparent method to the madness.

Shimoda City received over 5,000,000 tourists a year during its heyday, but once the bubble economy burst, the area saw a decrease in visitors, and many tourist businesses such as this one were forced to close down. Shimoda Fujiya Hotel, while located on prime real estate, had no parking lot, and the complex nature of the building made renovations costly, so after closing down it was left abandoned as-is. Nature has started to reclaim it, but if you sneak inside, you can still find all the old decorations left exactly where they were the day the hotel closed, like a mouldy time capsule back to the 1980s.

On the July 19, 2017 episode of *Sekai no Kowai Yoru* (Scary World Nights), comedian Sunshine Ikezaki (36) and actress Ryoga Haruhi (42) visited the hotel to find proof of ghosts. Supposedly, people who spend the night alone in room Mikomoto 38, the last room on the fourth floor, can hear a girl's voice and footsteps approaching the room.

As you may or may not know, the number four is unlucky in Japanese because it has the same pronunciation as the word for death, *shi*, so many public buildings will often skip naming their fourth floor as such and go straight to five, like Western buildings may skip the number thirteen. Yet the Shimoda Fujiya Hotel didn't, and now rumours abound that it's haunted.

The show claimed that a female staff member was possessed by a ghost whilst filming, although the spirit medium on hand was able to cleanse her of said spirits. They even managed to capture a supernatural presence on film as well, or so they claimed. Because the hotel remains in the same state it was originally in, it's easy and therefore popular for camera crews to film their variety shows there.

On September 29 of the same year, comedians Identity (Tajima Naoya, 34, and Miura Akihiko, 33) went to stay in the hotel for three nights and four days for a "I Lived In…" segment of the popular variety show *Bakumon Gakuen*. The pair were interrupted by a group of kids who entered the building for *kimodashi*, a popular ritual teenagers and young adults go through where they enter supposedly haunted locations to see how brave they really are, but once the kids saw them, they ran off. While the kids claimed they thought Miura was a "red-haired ghost," which is why they ran, the comedic duo were unable to catch anything supernatural on film during their brief stint living in the abandoned building.

In 2012, an anime called *Natsuiro Kiseki* was released. The anime was set in Shimoda and revolved around four young girls who were spending their potentially last summer together. In the show, there's a legend that if four close friends gather around a particular rock at a Shinto shrine and wish for the same thing, that wish will come true. The girls decide to try it and they discover that the legend is real. The tenth episode featured the girls visiting a haunted hotel, which is believed to be based on Shimoda's very own real-life haunted hotel, Shimoda Fujiya. The design is almost lifted whole-scale from the real building, right down to the location of the telegraph poles and rails.

It's unknown why the owners of the building haven't knocked it down entirely to build something new, but until then, Shimoda Fujiya Hotel is likely to remain one of the more popular ghost spots in Shizuoka, and a favourite for TV producers looking for a cheap scare.

Yellow House

Location: Hachijiri 95, Jimokuji, Ama City, Aichi Prefecture, 490-1111

It looked just like any other house. The yellow paint was a little tacky, and the triangle yard a little strange, but to anyone passing by on the busy street it was located in, it was just another family home.

Only it wasn't.

Rumours said that the house was built in the 1980s by a young husband and wife. But the husband was a prolific gambler, and before long, the couple were in huge debt. His wife pleaded for him to stop, but he didn't. They were in over their heads with nowhere left to go.

So the wife made a decision, and one night, after her husband returned home, she killed him and then took her own life. But that was only the beginning of the cursed house…

Little solid details are known about the so-called Yellow House in Aichi Prefecture. It goes by many names to the occult-loving public, but the Yellow House (thanks to its paint job) or the Triangle House (thanks to its triangular yard) are the most common.

The most popular story says that the house was built in the 1980s by a young couple. Details are scarce, and there are many variations to the story, but the most common version tells of a man who was unable to beat his gambling addiction, racking up a huge debt, and resulting in his wife murdering him before committing suicide, unable to take it any longer.

This was the start of what would be a long line of cursed families living in the house. Much like the infamous house in the *Ju-on* movies (and the house even came to be called the real-life *Ju-on*), just stepping inside could lead to being cursed.

The land the Yellow House was built on was once a cemetery, if the rumours are to be believed. At some point in the past, the graves were moved and the land put up for sale. An old woman opened up a small fruit and vegetable stall on the empty land, but she was evicted shortly thereafter and the land put up for sale as a residential spot. Rumours grew that memorial services were not held for the moved graves, however, and so the spirits continued to hang around even after the Yellow House was first built.

While the gambling story is the most common, other variations include a businessman who lost it all when the economic bubble burst, ending in a double suicide with his young wife because of their inability to pay back hefty loans. A slight variation on that story tells of only one of the couple committing suicide, while others have an entire family committing suicide in the house. Most stories tend to focus on the tragedy of a young husband and wife, however, and they always end with their deaths.

About five or six years after the first couple died in the house, it was said that another young couple moved in. They only lasted six months before moving out, and if you believe the rumours, it's because one of them went mad and was forced to be hospitalised. The lingering regret and malice of the first couple to die inside the Yellow House had not moved on.

The next couple to move in lasted a year before they also moved out. This continued over and over, with up to five different families moving into the house before moving out again a short time later. The shortest stay was only three days; the longest, one year. Was it truly the malice of that first couple forcing people out of their home, or something else?

This curse wasn't limited to the house's residents. Of the two police officers who visited the scene of the original crime, one ended up broken mentally and forced to live his time out in a hospital, while the other tried to take his own life. He was unsuccessful in his attempt and forced to live out the rest of his life disabled in a hospital.

There are also slight variations to the tale of the two police officers that went mad, however. In one version, they went to investigate the disappearance of an owner long after the original couple died. In this case, one officer went mad and was institutionalised while the other simply went missing and was never seen again.

Another version tells of three officers who visited the empty residence after receiving reports of shadowy figures on the second floor. They entered the house but were unable to find anything, but a short while later two of the officers went mad, while the other lost his memory and lived out the rest of his life as an invalid.

A third version tells of two officers visiting the

house after receiving a call from the owner of "poltergeist-like activity" taking place. The officers stayed overnight in the house to investigate, and as you may have guessed by now, one of the officers went mad and the other disappeared.

A more recent version tells of a group of teenagers entering the house for *kimodameshi*, a test of courage, and ending up possessed by spirits. The police were called in to investigate their strange actions and one officer ran towards the house screaming, "Who are you? Who are you?" But there was nobody there. The officer was later institutionalised.

Not enough police officers yet? Yet another version tells of a police officer visiting the house late at night after receiving reports of strange sounds. But a mere five minutes after entering the dark, empty house, he was seen fleeing the scene, screaming into the night.

It's not just police officers who are affected by the house. There are just as many versions that tell of teenagers and thrill seekers entering the house to see what all the fuss is about, only to end up going mad, possessed by ghosts, disappearing, or some combination of the above. The common theme running through all these stories is the same: enter the house and you will be cursed. In some cases, you may even die.

Another popular story tells of a spirit medium (in some versions, Gibo Aiko, who you can find in other ghost spots throughout this book) who visited the house to record a program on ghosts for TV. The moment the medium stood in front of the triangular yard, however, she froze. She refused to go in, and no amount of persuading would work. The program ended up being cancelled.

A slight variation to the same story reveals that the spirit medium did step foot inside the yard, but the moment she did, she started to act strange, and filming had to be cancelled in order to get her help. As a result, the medium ended up losing her memory.

There were even rumours that the horror drama *Damned File*, filmed by a nearby Nagoya TV station, tried to shoot an episode of the drama at the house, but ultimately were unable to enter. Perhaps for the best, considering what happened to everyone else who went inside.

These aren't the only stories. Over the years, rumours of the house grew and took on a life of their own, with the house becoming an urban legend in its own right. Supposedly, people who lived in the house heard tapping sounds when no-one was around, experienced poltergeist phenomena, heard the laughter of a child late at night on the second floor, saw shadows wandering the halls of the house at all hours, and even witnessed blood leaking from the shower.

After the house was abandoned, people reported seeing the pale face of a woman looking down at them from the second floor, and occasionally, a mother and child standing on the veranda. A mother holding her baby was seen on the front steps, and a baby's cries heard from the second floor. The spirits of a child and middle-aged man were seen by a rock in the garden, as well as that of an old lady wandering the empty house. Orbs were often seen floating in and around the house, and the sounds of footsteps heard in empty rooms. It was also said that if you took photos inside the building, you would be able to capture ghosts, and if you took your phone inside, it would stop working.

In 1996, an apartment complex was built next to the Yellow House lot. But if you believe the rumours, the curse isn't contained to the triangular yard, and the apartments had trouble keeping residents for any length of time on the first floor. Workers were then called in to destroy the Yellow House, but they were not immune either, and several reportedly went mad while others died on the job. Demolition of the house was then delayed.

One of the most famous features of the house was the blood-stained bed on the second floor. The house was left abandoned at some point with all the furniture inside. It was forbidden to trespass, and many tried to get permission over the years but were denied. This didn't stop teenagers looking for a thrill, however, and various videos made it to YouTube from their adventures inside the house. The blood-stained bed grew in fame, supposedly the site of the last murder in the house. There is, of course, no evidence that this is true, nor that the stain is even blood. Videos showed the state of the house at the time, which like many abandoned buildings, was falling apart at the seams.

Some lay the blame of the house's curse on the yard itself, and not the spirits that are said to reside there. The yard forms a triangle, not a square, and in Feng Shui, a triangular plot of land is said to be the worst. This triangle invites trouble into the house, particularly mental illness, and doesn't allow it to leave. Was the house doomed from the start? Or was it accident after accident that compounded to create the awful malice that ended up residing there by the end?

We may never truly know because in 2015, the Yellow House was finally torn down. The lot is now a parking lot, but depending on who you talk to, some report seeing the figure of a ghost loitering in the empty lot even today.

KANSAI

Kasagi Sightseeing Hotel

Location: Toge-50 Kasagi, Soraku District, Kyoto Prefecture, 619-1303

Before the Kasagi Tunnel was built, before the Lake Forest Resort was built, and before the Love Hotel Century was built, the Kasagi Sightseeing Hotel stood proud alongside the Kizu River in Kyoto Prefecture. Full of people and full of life, customer numbers began to dwindle when other, more easily accessible options opened up.

The hotel was rumoured to be in over 1,000,000 yen debt each month. Unable to deal with this sudden drop in guests and his rising money problems, the owner of the Kasagi Sightseeing Hotel walked down to the first floor, doused himself in oil and lit himself on fire. His attachment to his prized hotel was so strong, however, that even after death, he could not leave it. And he wasn't the only one.

They say the spirit of an old woman haunts the spiral stairs inside the building. If you're not careful, she'll throw you from them too.

On the roof, you'll find the disembodied head of a young woman, so dreadful that she chases all who see her to their grizzly ends. And every now and then, people lay eyes upon a former employee of the hotel, still in uniform and forever floating the halls of the now-abandoned building, looking for customers to help… or hinder.

These four spirits are the pillars of the haunted

Kasagi Sightseeing Hotel. Be careful if you ever try to visit, because it may be your last…

Located close to the borders of Kyoto, Nara, and Osaka Prefectures is the Kasagi Sightseeing Hotel. Situated at the end of a tiny path in the middle of the forest, it closed in 1990 thanks to the emergence of several easily accessible hotels nearby.

One of the most famous stories about the hotel is that the owner set himself on fire near the front entrance and killed himself. Ever since then, people claim to have seen the spirit of a burnt man wandering the building remains, and teenagers entering the building for a spot of midnight fun have reported leaving with burn marks on their own bodies. The building itself has been the subject of arson several times over the years, but there are some who claim that even these attacks were the work of the owner and not bored trespassers.

People report "a sensation like someone coming to greet you" upon entering the old building. One of the supposed "four pillars" of the Kasagi Sightseeing Hotel is a member of staff, although little information is known about this spirit or the person he was in life. People report seeing a man falling from the stairs to the ground, but there's no evidence that this is the same spirit.

The third of the four pillars, however, is said to reside on the staircase. Most of the stairways and floor have fallen apart or been torn down over the years, leaving a large atrium in the middle, and people claim that the spirit of an old woman resides here. Sometimes she's even seen with a little girl, although no-one knows who they are, exactly. It's likely they were once guests of the hotel before it was abandoned, but why they have taken up residence there now is unknown. Visitors to the abandoned building claim that if you look up into the giant gaping hole that was once the stairs, you can occasionally see a white figure looking back down. The area is also famous for floating orbs.

The fourth and most dangerous of the four pillars resides on the roof. Ghost hunters claim that from the fourth floor up, the atmosphere of the building completely changes. The roof now more often than not resembles a lake; water gathers in the rain and stagnates, unable to escape due to the concrete barriers surrounding it. As you may well know by now, Japanese spirits are attracted to water, so it makes sense that the most dangerous ghost of all would be found on the wet rooftop. Rumours abound that her bodiless head will chase anyone who sees her, and considering the state of the building now, that's almost a guaranteed death sentence.

This ghost became especially famous because of her appearance in *Kitano Makoto no Omaera Iku na Hishou Hen*, an occult video featuring the aforementioned comedian Kitano Makato. A young comedian from the Shouchiku Public Entertainment company was walking through the abandoned hotel when a woman's disembodied head was captured floating close behind him.

The building is, of course, off limits, but that doesn't stop people from entering. It has appeared on numerous TV shows over the years, thanks to the infamous ghost head sighting in Kitano Makato's video, and those with a strong ability to see the supernatural claim that the building can look like it is covered in fog at times; this is, in actuality, spirits that have come down from the mountains, attracted by the strong spiritual energy contained within the building.

The abandoned hotel has become so famous thanks to its TV appearances that locals have complained of the troubles that ghost hunters and kids looking for fun have caused. Because of them, the building is deteriorating even quicker, and that's not to mention all the people entering private property by mistake while looking for the hotel. A simple glance at the building reveals walls covered in graffiti, floors rotting and falling apart, and stairs coming apart at the seams. It may not be the Four Pillars of Kasagi Sightseeing Hotel that you really need to fear, but rather the dying building itself.

Genji Waterfall

Location: 2 Chome-15-1 Higashikuraji, Katano, Osaka Prefecture, 576-0061

It was New Year's Eve, and he hadn't seen his friends since high school a few years earlier. They went out drinking and eating, but there were still a few hours until midnight and the new year. They were bored.

"Wanna check out a ghost spot?"

Just like that, it was decided, and they went to visit the nearest place they could find: Genji Waterfall. A popular tourist attraction and, supposedly, the site of a tragic incident long ago. An incident that saw a young woman throw herself from the top of the waterfall, killing herself on the rocks below.

It was a long path through the forest to reach the waterfall, and on the way they passed a large collection of Jizo statues. He got the shivers. He remembered a story one of his friends told him about how his younger sister lost her scarf near the waterfall. On their way out, they found the scarf wrapped around one of the Jizo statue's necks. He turned away from them and pressed on.

They started walking up some stairs, but they seemed to go on forever. 'Are we ever going to reach the top? It has to be soon,' he thought, when suddenly his legs cramped up.

He was a soccer player and exercised every day. There was no way it was due to lack of exercise. He fell to his side and screamed out to his friends. "My legs! They're cramping!"

His friend turned to look at him, and his words chilled the blood in his veins.

"It looks like something's… pulling you…"

The young man panicked, but managed to drag himself to his feet. Pain spread throughout his legs like fire, but he did his best to ignore it. He didn't want to be there any longer. It wasn't right. There was something wrong about the place, and he wanted to get away as fast as possible… while he still could.

The group of friends arrived at the waterfall, and on their way back, the clock struck midnight. It was a new year. The pain in the young man's legs continued for several days after, but what worried him more than that, was the sensation of something pulling him down to the ground…

Located roughly 30 kilometres outside of Osaka City, Genji Waterfall can be found between the Kuraji Park and Katano City *Ikimono Fureai no Sato* (Animal Contact Park). The source of the waterfall is the Shirahata Pond in front of said park. Chosen as one of the eight most beautiful sights in Katano, and one of the top 100 greenest sites in Osaka, Genji Waterfall is overflowing with the beauty of nature and a popular hiking destination. While there is no public parking nearby, you can reach Genji Waterfall from Tsuda Station in about 25 minutes on foot.

Standing at 18 metres tall, it's said you can enjoy all four seasons by the waterfall. On the walk up the mountain you can enjoy the cherry blossoms during spring, the cool breeze during summer, the red leaves during autumn, and the snowfall during winter. Children often visit the area for school trips, and you can find tourists there all year round.

Katano is said to be the 'birthplace' of the Tanabata Star Festival myth, celebrated in Japan on July 7 each year. It is said to be the one day that literal star-crossed lovers Orihime and Kengyuu are able to meet over the Milky Way. A shrine dedicated to Orihime, Hatamono Shrine, can be found just a short distance away from Genji Waterfall. People come from all around to celebrate the festival, and Katano is said to receive over 700,000 tourists each year.

So how can such a bright and lively tourist attraction also function as a terrifying ghost spot?

There have long been rumours that a child fell from the top of the waterfall and died. When night falls, the child's spirit can be seen wandering around the area. And regardless of whether it's day or night, there have been multiple eyewitness reports over the years of *hitodama*—supernatural glowing lights said to be souls—around the waterfall. It's also a good spot to try to capture some ghost photography, as many people over the years have claimed to have captured spirits on film in the area, particularly in the toilets close to the waterfall.

But there's another, much older, story that has been passed down over the years that tells of how Genji Waterfall got its name.

Long ago, in the village of Katano, there lived a

beautiful young lady called Genji-hime. She lived together with her cute younger brother, Umechiyo. They were not blood relatives, but ever since a young age they had been living together. Both children had lost their mother, and so found kinship with each other.

There was a mountain on the border of Kawachi and Yamato called Mount Orochi, and on that mountain there lived a group of bandits. Every now and then the bandits would come down from the mountains and pillage the nearby homes, running amok and doing whatever they liked.

As the year was coming to an end, the bandits finally made their appearance in the village of Katano. They attacked Genji's residence, and along with her brother Umechiyo, she was tied up and taken away.

The subordinates informed their boss that they'd captured a beautiful young girl and a young boy. The boss, a beautiful woman in her forties, told them to bring the pair at once. Yet the boy was so shocked at the surprise attack that when they brought him to her, he was already dead.

The boss stared at the young boy, her complexion suddenly changing, and she told her subordinates to leave. As they moved to a different room, the boss quickly untied Genji and then cried over the lifeless body of Umechiyo. Genji was suspicious of the woman's strange actions, but seeing her cute brother dead, she could hold it in no longer.

"Know that you are the enemy of my brother!" Genji screamed. She sprang upon the woman with a short dagger and thrust it into her chest. But the woman did not resist her. Instead, she gripped Genji's hand, and as tears streamed down her face she screamed, "Genji-hime, Umechiyo, please forgive me."

Genji was astonished at such unexpected words from the mouth of her enemy. The boss then informed Genji that she was her real mother. When she was younger, she was married and gave birth to a daughter, but due to certain circumstances, she was forced to give the child up and leave. She later married again, this time giving birth to a young boy, Umechiyo, although she was once again forced to give the child up and leave.

18 years then passed, and her two children weighed heavily on her mind. Although she was a bandit, she wished just once to meet her children again. It was through a sad coincidence that today was that day, under unexpected circumstances that saw them dead and dying at each other's hands. While Genji and Umechiyo had only lived as pretend brother and sister, they were in fact children born to the same woman, the boss of the bandits.

How sad Genji was, having killed her mother by her own hand. She cried over the bodies of her mother and younger brother, and unable to deal with what happened, she threw herself over a nearby waterfall. And so, Genji-hime followed her mother and brother into the afterlife.

Close to the waterfall there is a large rock called the *Yonaki Ishi*, or crying stone. Legend states that after Genji threw herself from the waterfall, people could hear her sobs coming from the stone night after night. The area is now surrounded with stone Buddha statues to appease her spirit and help her move on, but still people continue to hear her cries as night falls.

You can find numerous statues of the Buddhist guardian Jizo at the bottom of the waterfall, as well as several rock towers. Jizo is said to guide spirits into the afterlife, especially children who die before they're able to build any karma in life. The spirits of children who die before their parents are said to be doomed to stack rocks on the shores of the Sanzu River each day to build karma, only to have demons come out of the river and knock them down each night. By building those rock stacks, it's thought to reduce the time needed for children to do so on the other side.

Genji Waterfall and its surrounding areas are a particularly religious area, having once been a Buddhist training ground. It's also a prime example of Japan's gift of melding the old with the new. A mix of bittersweet fairy tale with haunting modern ghosts.

Kaizuka Tuberculosis Clinic

Location: 1175 Jizodo, Kaizuka, Osaka Prefecture, 597-0053

They went in three cars. A group of 11 on their way to the abandoned Kaizuka Tuberculosis Clinic. They were well prepared. They did their research on the building and took with them flashlights and salt. Just in case.

There was something about the building that attracted them to it. The blackened walls and broken glass just screamed "Look at me! I'm abandoned! Come explore my innards!"

The bright lights of Osaka dimmed suddenly as they turned the corner towards the old hospital. Before them was nothing but darkness, almost like they'd entered another dimension. It was just past 2 a.m. when they pulled into the driveway, and what stood before them in the black of night was the perfect haunted hospital. They were here.

They pulled their cars up in front of the hospital and, one by one, got out to marvel at it. The hospital was split into two different buildings, both overgrown with weeds. The left was the dining hall, the right the hospital. That's what they assumed, anyway. They made their way towards the right.

What they found inside was exactly what they expected. Broken glass littered the floor, and they had to step over trash and broken furniture to get anywhere. The place was a mess. They found old x-rays and patient photos, and even a register of names. It was like everyone just up and disappeared.

The group made their way to the second floor. The hallway was dark. Too dark. Something told them they shouldn't go down there. One of the guys, who possessed a strong ability to sense the supernatural, put his hand out and stopped the group.

"There's someone down there. He's been watching us since we came in."

Nobody else could see him.

"Did you hear that?"

They didn't.

"He just said something. It sounded like… 'Hey.'"

His friends laughed and slapped him on the shoulder. They thought he was just messing with them, or perhaps he had confused the sound of their footsteps.

But then they heard it too.

"Hey!"

The group ran, the sound echoing off the walls as they fled to their cars. The sound continued as they drove home, echoing over and over inside their heads.

"Hey…!"

The Kaizuka Tuberculosis Clinic in Osaka first opened in 1948 as a boys' home for young children recovering from medical treatment. In 1958, it officially became a tuberculosis centre, and it operated until 1992, when the clinic was closed. Tuberculosis had become less common, and patients fewer and fewer. There was little need for the clinic to remain open, and so it was abandoned.

Many young children died in the clinic over the 44 years it ran, often painfully and slowly. Once the hospital was abandoned, it didn't take long for it to become a regular hunting ground for those looking to experience a creepy night out, or perhaps find some evidence of the ghosts that were surely left behind.

It quickly became a well-known ghost spot, and its location in a quiet, dark, residential area made it the perfect location for some late night ghost hunting. The owners even left everything inside when they closed the hospital, creating an undeniable spooky atmosphere as people walked through hospital rooms and doctors' offices left as-is. The x-rays and patient photos scattered around the building sealed the deal. If you wanted to see a ghost, you had to go to Kaizuka Tuberculosis Clinic.

But having said that, solid stories of the ghosts that exist there are few and far between. The clinic is another good example of a place that has become haunted not because of any one particular accident, but simply because of its tragic history. There was no gruesome murder that hit the news and made the site famous overnight. There was no one particular ghost that people claimed to see whenever they visited. Instead, it was a variety of ghosts. An atmosphere, if you will, that the place was haunted, even if there was no real story behind it.

In 2015, the hospital was finally demolished, although the boys' dorm remained. What were the spirits to do now that their home was gone? How were they going to haunt people, or complain about their horrid afterlife? People claimed that the ghosts moved over to the boys' dorms once the hospital was destroyed. Why haunt an empty lot when there was a perfectly good abandoned building right next door?

In 2017, an Italian restaurant called *Mori no Komichi*, or Small Forest Lane, was built on the site of the old hospital. You can visit the restaurant today and enjoy a nice Italian meal where ghosts supposedly once roamed. But if you can't fight it any longer and absolutely must see the ghosts, remember: they've just moved next door.

Sandanbeki Cliffs

Location: 2927-52 Shirahama-cho, Nishimuro District, Wakayama Prefecture, 649-2211

They said that the spirits called from the ocean depths below. They said the spirits crawled up the cliff face to grab people and drag them to their doom. They said that you would be overcome with an overwhelming urge to jump if you stood too close to the edge.

As she looked out over the sea, at the jagged rocks jutting out of the water and the waves crashing against the hard stone wall, suddenly she understood. She closed her eyes, and there it was. A voice in the back of her head.

'If you jump, all your problems will float away. There will be no more pain. Nothing.'

The thought crossed her mind just briefly. No more pain. That would be nice. Just let it all end. Peace and quiet sounded wonderful.

She took a step towards the edge. And then another. Her body was moving by itself, and she let it.

"Shit!"

She flung her eyes open and ran. What the hell was that? She didn't want to jump. She didn't want it all to end. So what was that feeling that overcame her all of a sudden?

Were the rumours actually true…?

"Sandanbeki is a massive rock formation that stretches for 2km along the coast and resembles a

Japanese folding screen. The cliffs are approximately 35m tall (41m at the highest point), and once were used by fishermen keeping a lookout for schools of fish."

So reads the sign situated before the Sandanbeki Cliffs in Wakayama Prefecture, located in one of the most southernmost reaches of the island of Honshu. But it's not the only sign located at the cliffs. There's another, much more dire sign located close to the cliff's edge.

"PHONE LIFELINE
In my eyes, you have value and are irreplaceable. I love you.
Jesus said, 'I am the light. Those who follow me will never walk in darkness, but will carry with them the light of life.'-*Holy Bible*
Before you make such an important decision, please call us to talk. We'll be waiting for you.
Shirahama Baptist Christian Church."

Known as one of the most beautiful sights in Japan, Sandanbeki also has a dark side to it; it's also a famous suicide spot. On June 10, 1950, a young couple made their way to Sandanbeki. They wished to get married, but their parents rejected them. Not wishing to be parted, they left their final message on a nearby rock in lipstick: "Today, too, the waves of Shirahama are stormy." They then threw themselves from the cliffs in a double suicide.

A year later, a friend of the couple returned to the very same rock and carved their final message into its face so it wouldn't be lost to the annals of time. All they wanted was to be together, but they were unable to achieve that in life. In death, however, they could be together forever. A rumour started to spread that couples who touched the rock would be able to spend their futures together in happiness, or that if you touched the rock with the person you liked, they would also fall in love with you.

In April 2016, the spot came to be known as the "Lovers' Holy Ground," and couples from all over visit it each year to take wedding photos or go on dates. It may seem a little morbid to celebrate your love on the very spot two young people killed themselves because they could not, but nevertheless, the Lovers' Holy Ground is an unmissable attraction if you're serious about your relationship. On June 12, 2016, almost 76 years to the day that the couple threw themselves from the Sandanbeki Cliffs, "Lovers' Day" was announced and a heart monument erected by the Lovers' Holy Ground viewing platform. There you can leave a heart-shaped padlock signifying your love is forever, available for a small price from a store nearby.

But while couples frequently visit the cliffs to celebrate their love, many others visit it for another reason. The same reason the original couple did; to end their lives. A stone monument stands before the cliffs in commemoration of those who lost their lives in shipwrecks around the coast, and also those who willingly took their own lives by throwing themselves into the sea below.

In 2013, the *Shuukan Post* published an article about the taxi drivers who often delivered people to their deaths at the Sandanbeki Cliffs.

"Where is your hotel?" the taxi driver asked a woman in her late 20s as she got into his cab.

"I don't have one. I'm here to meet someone."

The driver pulled up in front of the PHONE LIFELINE sign. Male, female, young, old. Those who arrive in Shirahama without luggage are only ever visiting the cliffs for one reason. All it takes is one step forward, and that's it. It's all over.

"If you're in trouble, please give me a call," the driver told the woman. She hid behind her hair and refused his business card. If the driver contacted his company over the wireless, they would soon send the police out. But as the woman walked away, she waved to someone on the path. She really was meeting up with someone. The driver was relieved.

The next day, he got a call from the police.

"Did you pick up this woman yesterday?"

She was dead, her body found on the rocks at the bottom of the cliffs. Those who take their lives at the cliffs don't necessarily end up in the ocean; most end up on the jagged rocks below, leaving their broken bodies to be recovered by rescue teams.

The driver remembered that the woman was wearing a brown blouse, and she got out at precisely 10:38 a.m. In a single month, the driver would deliver perhaps two or three people to the cliffs who were looking to end their lives. Not everyone would go through with it, but as much as he could try to lend a helping hand, or willing ear, there was nothing he could do if they were not willing to accept it.

Around 20 people commit suicide at the Sandanbeki Cliffs each year. While that number has been decreasing in recent years, thanks to regular patrols and the efforts of the community to help those who are at the end of their rope, it still remains a popular spot for people looking to end it all.

A man who ran a souvenir shop in front of the cliffs told the *Shuukan Post* that "When you talk to people who are about to end their lives, they always say they're here to 'meet someone.' Just who exactly are they supposed to be meeting here, of all places? I call out to perhaps 100 people a year. Amongst those, there are people who don't want to die. It's important to first talk to them."

It has been said that the spirits of those who have already taken their lives call to people standing on the cliffs from below. They beckon them to join them, and their siren's call can be almost unbearable for those who are looking for a reason to end their suffering.

Beneath the Sandanbeki Cliffs lie the Sandanbeki Caves. You can take an elevator from the viewing platform roughly 36 metres underground, and there you'll find a walkway roughly 200 metres long where you can stroll the dark, wet caves. During the Genpei War (1180-1185), the Kumano Navy—led by Kumano Betto, the father of Benkei, one of Japan's most famous warrior monks—took refuge in the caves. They have a long history, and much of it dark. Ghost photos are not uncommon in the caves, with people returning to find strange orbs in their photos that they never noticed, or even occasionally a *namakubi*, or freshly severed ghost head.

One spirit medium from the *Gibo Kantei Office* claimed that a married couple brought her a photo they had taken at the cliffs. In it was the floating head of a woman with long hair surrounded by several orbs. The couple feared they were cursed because they had fallen ill since visiting the cliffs, and it had even spread to their son, who had a bike accident and broke his arm.

The medium viewed footage the couple had shot in the caves and discovered "incalculable spirits of the dead" swimming around the foot of the cliffs. She claimed they were "acting as one" and had become something more than just spirits; they were more akin to the living embodiment of malice, an evil that wanted nothing more than to pull even more living souls down from the cliffs into the depths below.

The Sandanbeki Cliffs may be beautiful, and they should definitely be on your to-see list when in Japan, but they also harbour a dark side. You should always take care when visiting, and be mindful of what is going on around you.

"It is not a place you should visit if you are feeling lost or have serious problems. If you're not careful, you will be dragged over to the other side."

CHUGOKU

Manohara Mountain Villa

Location: Prefectural Road 45, Myoko, Sekigane-cho, Kurayoshi City, Tottori Prefecture, 682-0423

Two teens from the same cram school were bored one day and decided to go visit the local "*Yurei* Hotel." Maybe some ghosts would liven their day. It was a little out of the way—an abandoned hotel sitting in the middle of nowhere—but if it killed their boredom, it would be worth it.

When they got there, they were less than impressed, however. It was just a plain old abandoned building. It didn't give off any haunted vibes, it was just old and covered in overgrown weeds.

They stepped through the tall grass, but the moment they did, it was like they stepped into another dimension. Everything felt different. They were standing in the same spot, but it was like they stepped through an invisible curtain and everything was wrong.

The two pushed on. A strange feeling wasn't enough to deter them from their explorations. They stepped inside the first building they saw. The roof was falling down, and the walls falling apart. They couldn't see anything, but warning sirens were blaring inside their heads.

They had to get out. Something was wrong with the place. The pair fled the building at the same time. They ran all the way back to the street, hearts pounding wildly.

That place was dangerous. They couldn't put their fingers on why, exactly, but something stuck out like a sore thumb. The building was a mess. Literally falling apart. So why hadn't anyone knocked it down yet...?

Lying in the shadow of Mount Daisen, the tallest mountain in the Chugoku Region, sits several tiny, abandoned buildings in the middle of nowhere. Surrounded by thick forests, numerous rice fields, and very little else, these buildings were once known as the "Manohara Mountain Villa Hotel (Sauna Attached)." These days, however, it's better known to the locals as the "Yurei Hotel."

Draped in fog that constantly rolls down from the mountains, you might be forgiven for thinking you've stepped into *Silent Hill*, or perhaps more appropriately, *Forbidden Siren*. An old-fashioned sign mounted on metal pipes, not unlike that of a tower you might see in *Forbidden Siren*, rises high into the sky, letting you know that you have arrived at the "Sauna Attached Hotel." That is, if you can now locate it amongst the overgrown trees and untended branches that obscure it from sight. The rest of the sign lies broken and abandoned in the forest, much like the villa itself.

As the name suggests, the Manohara Mountain Villa is made up of several buildings. There is the two-story administrative building, and then a short distance away, past the garage, you'll find the lodgings—which, of course, come with a sauna attached. A quick look inside lets you know that you're not dealing with just any old hotel, however.

The narrow rooms, bright red walls and gaudy furniture all scream love hotel. That's right; the Manohara Mountain Villa, hidden deep at the foot of the mountains in the middle of nowhere, is a love hotel. Or, *was* a love hotel.

It's uncertain when exactly it went out of business, but in 1991, the local *Nihonkai Newspaper* published an article stating that the abandoned hotel was haunted. Ever since then, rumours spread and it came to be feared as the "Yurei Hotel" by locals.

One of the ghosts that haunts the hotel is said to appear in the administrative building. A quick step inside and it's not hard to see why. The outside is covered in graffiti, and all the window and door glass is broken, but inside is even worse.

The second-story floor has collapsed due to rot, leaving a giant, gaping hole in the roof. Furniture has fallen down and remained where it landed; cabinets, an old TV, metal poles and other furniture lay in a pile where they fell, and an old vacuum was once found hanging in mid-air. Not by ghostly powers, but simply because its cords got stuck and there it remained, swaying in the middle of the room. The outside walls from the second floor have also been ripped off over the years, leaving the building just barely standing.

Over in the lodgings, the ghost of a young woman is said to appear. Was she a visitor to the hotel? The victim of violence, left to haunt the building she was murdered in? Or was she a local who found herself attracted to the spiritual energy of the building, taking up residence with the other ghosts in the popular Yurei Hotel? Details are scarce, and the real answer likely lies in the fact that someone once claimed the hotel was haunted, thus, the ghost of a young woman must lurk its corridors. What's a haunted building without its obligatory female ghost, after all?

The Manohara Mountain Villa is small enough that you can explore the entire lot within 20 minutes. Finding it may take a little longer, however, because even with a map, Manohara is so out of the way that you might need a little spiritual guidance to even get there in the first place.

Kamome Manor

Location: Prefectural Road 29, Taisha-cho Hinomisaki, Izumo City, Shimane Prefecture, 699-0763

She was 20 at the time and on a date with her boyfriend when he told her he wanted to visit Kamome Manor. They were on their way to Hinomisaki Lighthouse to do a little sightseeing when he suggested the detour.

"My friend said there really are ghosts there, so what do you say? Wanna go?"

She refused, but he wouldn't take no for an answer, so they compromised. They could go, but only while it was still daytime. There was no way she would go at night. Whether there were ghosts there or not, the place was creepy. She didn't want to be there in the dark.

They pulled up in front of the manor and got out to have a look. Even in the daylight it was dark and gloomy, and the wind blowing in from the ocean behind it was freezing. She hesitated before stepping inside.

The walls were covered in graffiti and the place was a mess. Her boyfriend took the lead, not afraid of anything. He researched the place beforehand and knew that the basement was especially famous for ghosts, so they walked around together, looking for the stairs.

"Is this them?" he said about five minutes later. She looked over and the moment she saw them, she froze. Her skin broke out into goosebumps.

"We can't go down there," she said. "We gotta get out of here! Right now!"

She ran, dragging her boyfriend to the exit. A voice rang out from behind them, like someone moaning.

"Did you hear that?" she asked.

"I don't hear anything!" her boyfriend replied.

"It doesn't matter. We just need to get out of here!"

She ran back to the car at full speed and they took off. The moment they were off the manor grounds, it was like the oppressive air surrounding them dissipated. When they were far away, and she was calmed down, she asked her boyfriend to show her the photos he had taken. She told him not to take any at the time, but now she was curious. Perhaps he captured whatever was making that sound.

The building was covered in orbs. Left, right, here, there, everywhere. All over the building. The couple looked at each other.

Then her blood ran cold again. Looking closer, she could see the face of a woman looking right at them from the window…

Kamome means seagull in Japanese, and fittingly, this large manor sits very close to the cliffs facing the Sea of Japan in Izumo, Shimane Prefecture. This two-story building bends like an L shape in the middle, and from its open, flat roof you have a clear view of the ocean and surrounding forest.

While it's only a two or three-minute drive from Hinomisaki Shrine (a supposed spiritual power spot), Kamome Manor sits almost completely isolated from civilisation. Behind it is the Sea of Japan, and to the front and sides, nothing but forest and mountains. There is a single road leading to the manor—now blocked off—that can be found on Prefectural Road 29. It's the perfect location for ghost stories, and it comes with more than just a few.

There are various rumours about what Kamome Manor used to be. It was a hospital, a hotel, an old peoples' home, it was actually a secret location where sinister human experimentation took place; it was even a sanatorium. Yet as the name would suggest, Kamome Manor was an inn.

Due to its unfavourable location, it closed approximately 30 years ago. There were rumours that when contractors tried to demolish the building, they were plagued with accidents and so many unlucky incidents that, in the end, they gave up, judging it too dangerous. Ever since then, the building has been left as-is, and now it's a popular ghost spot.

As is common with other abandoned buildings, the manor has been ransacked, vandalised, and otherwise abused over the years. Its location and relative ease of access make it the perfect spot for thrill seekers or kids looking to go wild for the night. But those who are thinking of visiting Kamome Manor should perhaps think twice about whether it's worth it or not. There are a lot of rumours about the manor, and none of them are good.

Perhaps the most famous of all involves well-known psychic and medium Gibo Aiko. Gibo first appeared on TV in 1961, and over the next forty years she appeared in a variety of shows as a spiritual counsellor. She also wrote several best-selling books over the years.

Shortly before her death, Gibo visited Kamome Manor for a certain TV show. When she arrived, however, Gibo was said to have exclaimed there were so many spirits in the area that she was unable to perform an exorcism for them all. Terrified and powerless to do anything, she left. A month later, she died. The official cause was stomach cancer, but many have claimed that she was just one of many to have been cursed by visiting Kamome Manor.

It's said that those who visit Kamome Manor either die or face serious injury upon their return home. One story tells of a young man who visited the manor with his girlfriend and another friend. They drove from Matsue, roughly 40 minutes away, telling ghost stories the whole way. They made their way into the manor, spraying graffiti and looking around.

There have long been rumours that those who enter the basement will return vomiting blood, fall ill to pneumonia and high fevers, then be subjected to nightmares and the voice of a child screaming long after they return home. There's even said to be a forbidden door that no-one can open. Aware of these rumours, the trio decided to leave the basement until last for the ultimate scary experience.

They made their way around the first and second floors, but found nothing of note. They went to the roof and the young man told his friend to scream something into the empty void. He didn't want to go home without something of note happening. His friend screamed out, "O~~~i!" and a deep voice from the earth returned the call. The trio panicked and fled the building.

On the way home, they passed a dead kitten as they drove through a tunnel. They swerved to avoid it, and a short while later the friend started to complain.

"Stop it. You're freaking me out!"

When the young man asked him what was going on, his friend complained that he kept touching his knee. But the young man was sitting in the passenger's seat, and his friend was sitting in the back behind the driver. Not only that, his friend complained that he was touching his right knee. The driver's side is on the right in Japanese cars, so that would make it impossible for him to reach from the passenger's side in the front without everyone seeing him. When he pressed his friend further, he said whatever touched him was about the size of a child's hand.

Thinking it might be the work of the dead kitten, the young man told his girlfriend to turn around so they could get it and deliver it to a place full of people. She did as instructed, but then she suddenly turned the steering wheel and the car ploughed into a house. The three were lucky to escape without serious injuries, but the car was totalled. When the young man later asked his girlfriend what happened, she claimed a white orb had crossed their path, so she swerved to avoid it.

Other ghostly rumours of the manor say there is a large collection of bones buried beneath the building. Some have claimed a woman drowned herself in the sea by the cliffs during the Meiji Era, and her ghost haunts the building to this day. Others say there are the spirits of an old man and child, and even more say you can hear the high-pitched laughter of a woman inside the manor's walls, and a man's screams from a room on the second floor.

The manor is also a popular spot for ghost photos, as you're supposed to be able to capture ghostly orbs and other spiritual phenomena at the manor even during broad daylight.

Less ghostly rumours suggest the manor is used by the yakuza for their shady dealings. There have even been rumours that the building was used by North Korean spies over the years. Whether any of these are true or not, it's generally a good idea not to go exploring dark, abandoned buildings in the middle of nowhere, especially those with such an unsavoury reputation—supernatural or otherwise—as Kamome Manor.

House of Talismans

Location: 3136 Kojimayuga, Kurashiki City, Okayama Prefecture, 711-0901

They called it the scariest ghost spot in all of Okayama. A home that was the site of a family suicide. The events that took place there that night were so awful, so violent, that the relatives sought help from a monk to assist the family's spirits in moving onto heaven. But the monk was unable to do anything, and as a last resort, he left talismans all over the house, instead sealing the spirits inside.

A group of friends heard about the infamous "House of Talismans" and decided to film a YouTube video there. They gathered their equipment, jumped in the car, and made their way to the outskirts of Kurashiki City. The house sat in the middle of nowhere, alone in a sea of trees and surrounded by swampland. The atmosphere as they drove up the path towards the house was dark, gloomy, and oppressive. Perfect to film some creepy video.

Yet as the friends stood before the house, their laughter suddenly died. The sight of it sent shivers down their spines. It was right there, and it was real. Something about it was creepy and off-putting, but that was exactly what they were after, so they stepped inside.

They turned their cameras on and walked around the remains of the house. It looked lived in, despite its deterioration. Dishes littered the sink, furniture from the family that lived there remained in its original location, and clothes lay strewn all over the floor. But as they were filming, they suddenly heard a noise from the next room.

Bang!

They looked at each other. What was that? They didn't see signs of anyone else in the house when they arrived. They nervously approached the next room and looked inside. Judging by the sound of the noise, something large had fallen over. Yet there was nothing there. Nothing that could have made the noise, anyway.

They continued with their filming, but then one of the members started to feel unwell. He couldn't stop shaking. Fearing the worst, the friends got back in the car. They started back towards civilisation, but on the way, they heard another noise.

Bang!

This time it was the back of the car, but again, they couldn't see anything. Their friend continued to shake. Was he possessed? Had something come along for the ride with him?

The young man was starting to rant and rave, clearly at his wit's end. They couldn't leave him alone, so the friends drove to a nearby convenience store and waited the night out with him. But when they finally took him home the next morning, he fell ill. He was sick for an entire week, and it wasn't until they took him to be purified that he got better…

The "House of Talismans," as it is commonly called these days, is a family home on the outskirts of Kurashiki City in Okayama Prefecture. It is a lone house with no neighbours, surrounded by nothing but trees. It is also abandoned, and has been for many years.

The story goes that the family who lived there committed suicide. All at once. Nobody knows why, but after they did, strange phenomena started to occur in the area. Relatives of the family visited a monk in the hopes of ending the bizarre occurrences, but he was unable to help the spirits and so he sealed the house with talismans instead.

Most of the talismans have been torn down thanks to people visiting the house for *kimodameshi*, but some still remain scattered around the remains of the house. The building is in poor condition, but like many other abandoned homes, the furniture and household items remain, giving the house an eerie lived-in feel, despite its state of disrepair.

The internet is full of tales of people who visited the house to test their courage, only to fall ill after returning. Even tales of the family suicide are only hearsay; nobody knows the real reason why the house was abandoned or why it was covered in talismans, but a large number of people claim to feel sick after visiting. Whether this is mental or something more sinister, who knows?

One spirit medium who visited the house claimed that, contrary to the story of the family suicide, the house was the home of a religious sect. The talismans were hung up to purify the building, but they had no effect because "they didn't purify the energy of the area." The bad energy of the house attracted spirits, and whether there was a mass suicide in the house or not, it became a gathering spot for dark spirits from all around.

Rumours say that if you visit the house at night, you'll be cursed. Whether you believe in curses or not, it remains solid advice. If you stumble and injure yourself in the House of Talismans, help is a long way away, and you might find yourself with nothing but angry spirits for company until it arrives.

Motoujina Lighthouse

Location: 24 Motoujina-machi, Minami Ward, Hiroshima City, Hiroshima Prefecture, 734-0012

It was night, and they were taking a break by the famous Motoujina Park. The air was cool and the scenery beautiful, and in the distance they could hear the waves crashing against the beach of Hiroshima Bay.

They were sitting in the car park when a cat walked by. The girlfriend picked it up and patted it, showing it to her boyfriend. There was also a dog nearby, but it didn't show any signs of movement.

She carried the cat with her as they walked down towards the lighthouse. The dog followed at a safe distance, but then suddenly it dropped to its haunches and started growling. The cat popped its claws, hissed, and jumped down. The woman looked at her boyfriend, eyes wide. Animals were sensitive. Everyone knew that. They could see things the human eye couldn't.

There had long been rumours that the tree in front of the lighthouse was a popular suicide spot. But neither of them could see anything. Could the animals?

Her blood ran cold. If the animals hadn't been with them, and if they'd continued on their way, what would they have encountered down there?

They turned to return to the car. Both the dog and cat were gone…

Motoujina Lighthouse can be found on the southern

tip of Ujina Island overlooking Hiroshima Bay. The light of the lighthouse stands 45 metres above sea level, while the lighthouse itself is roughly 21 metres high. The lights first turned on in 1950, and while the lamps have since been replaced, the lens is still the original Fresnel lens made in France in 1895. The lighthouse stands tall as a symbol of the Motoujina Park that lies at its feet, and continues to safely guide ships into Hiroshima Bay today.

Yet Motoujina Lighthouse is also one of the most famous ghost spots in Hiroshima. There's a large, 300-year-old camphor tree in front of the lighthouse where it's said that numerous people have committed suicide over the years. Japan has a rather high suicide rate, with close to 30,000 people taking their lives each year. Only recently has that number started to decline, but the problem remains prolific, and in Hiroshima, Motoujina Lighthouse was once a popular spot for those looking to end their pain.

The ghosts of those who took their lives supposedly loiter in the nearby park and parking lot, and people claim to have seen ghosts in the public toilets as well. One of the more famous rumours speaks of a female ghost that crawls around on all fours inside the toilets.

Another popular rumour about the area states that if you take a photo of the camphor tree, the developed photos will show a hazy figure, or even that the photos will develop half-red. Japanese ghosts love to hang around watery areas, and with Motoujina Lighthouse sitting right on the edge of Hiroshima Bay, it makes it the perfect spot for ghost rumours to brew.

During the day, the park beneath Motoujina Lighthouse is a popular spot for businessmen to take a break from their busy workday, and tourists come from all around to visit the area. There's even a hotel only a few hundred metres from the lighthouse. The sound of the waves from the bay and the wind rustling through the trees is a breath of fresh air from the hustle and bustle of city life.

Yet, come night-time, the park is closed, and entrance to the area near the lighthouse is forbidden. While some claim this was done to stop people from killing themselves by the large camphor tree, officially the area is closed at night because it was a popular gathering spot for delinquents up to no good.

Either way, Motoujina Lighthouse and its surrounding park are not an area you want to be in come nightfall. While the lighthouse is busy guiding boats to safety, spirits may be busy trying to guide people somewhere else.

Ookunoshima

Location: Tadanoumi-cho, Takehara City, Hiroshima Prefecture, 729-2311

A young man visited a small island off the coast of Hiroshima called Ookunoshima with his friend. They had a summer holidays project, as is the norm for most Japanese school students, so they visited the island to do some research.

Having finished what they came to do, the two friends decided to explore the island. It was a rare opportunity, after all, and it was well known for its abandoned buildings and wild rabbit population. It wasn't long before the pair found themselves in an unpopulated area away from the rest of the island's tourists.

While they were walking, the young man's friend got his foot stuck in a tree root and fell over. A kind figure offered a hand to help him up; he gratefully accepted.

"A-ah, thank you," his friend said. As he stood up, he noticed that the man standing before him was strangely wearing a Japanese Imperial Army uniform. Not only that, a gas mask was covering his face. But Japan didn't have an army; it was abolished when they surrendered at the end of the Second World War. The sight of a man standing before him in a gas mask and uniform that no longer existed terrified him. The young man and his friend ran in terror.

But as they ran, another soldier came running towards them wielding a katana.

"You better hurry away from here, quickly!" the soldier in the gas mask yelled after them. The duo didn't need to be told twice; they took off as fast as their feet would carry them, back to a populated area of the island. But who were the men, and why did they have such old weapons of war? And why was that soldier in the gas mask so kind to them in the first place…?

Ookunoshima is a small island located to the southwest of Hiroshima in the Inland Sea of Japan, roughly 3 kilometres from the mainland and 4.3 kilometres in circumference. You can reach the island by ferry from Tadanoumi on the mainland in the north, or from Omishima Island in the south.

These days it's affectionately known as *Usagi Shima* (Rabbit Island) because of the large number of wild rabbits that roam the island. It's said that over 800 rabbits now inhabit Ookunoshima, released onto the island after the Second World War when it was being developed as a national park, and they are so friendly that they often come right up to visitors to say hello. So, how could such a cute place be known as a terrifying ghost spot?

The Chinese characters used to spell "Ookunoshima" mean "large, old field island." Yet at one point in its past, people used a different set of characters when referring to it. They referred to it using the characters for "large painful island," which read exactly the same way: Ookunoshima.

In 1925, Japan signed the Geneva Protocol which banned the usage of chemical warfare. In the same year, the Imperial Japanese Army began its secret program to develop chemical weapons. Starting in 1927 and completed in 1929, a chemical munitions plant was built on Ookunoshima, and it was used to manufacture poisonous gases until the end of the Second World War.

The workers wore gas masks and other protective clothing, but they weren't yet skilled in the manufacture of poisonous gases, and lacked the materials required to do so safely. There were many accidents, and over 300 people died during their time on the island. When taking into account the after-effects the gas had on the workers, more than 3,000 people died overall.

Of the 6,600 people that worked on the island during the war, it's said that more than 4,200 of them ended up in hospital in the years that followed. For this reason, the island was even eliminated from Japanese maps, and what happened there kept a secret from the public.

It's been said that Ookunoshima produced 30,000 tons of poison gas and over 16,000 gas bombs. At the end of the war, the army tried to dismantle the production factory quickly to hide all evidence of its existence, and some have claimed that in their haste, the army dumped many of the weapons straight into the sea, rather than disposing of them properly. The rest was incinerated. Blackened buildings remain to this day, and there are still parts of the island today where the soil is so contaminated that people are forbidden to enter.

But it is also said that if you take photos in these areas, you can find ghosts in them once developed. In particular, many people say you can see a white ghost in one of the abandoned buildings on the island. Because of the effects of the poisonous gas production, and the state of the world at the time, many people died with regret in their hearts and have been unable to pass on to heaven, lingering on the island as spirits.

A poison gas museum was opened on the island in 1988 "in order to alert as many people as possible to the dreadful truths about poison gas." The museum curator has been quoted as saying he wishes for people to understand that the Japanese were both aggressors and victims during the war.

Hiroshima City and the Atomic Bomb Dome—perhaps the greatest sign of the pain Japan suffered during the Second World War—sit just a few kilometres away on the mainland. But head a few islands over to Ookunoshima, the large island of pain, and you can see the flip side of that coin. A place where Japan itself also committed war crimes. A place where the spirits are still suffering from what took place there close to a century ago.

SHIKOKU

Mother and Child Gravesite

Location: 1916-3 Kouchi, Mugi City, Ama District, Tokushima Prefecture, 775-0001

"Turn Hose into fields, turn it into a heap.
50 years after my death, Hose shall be destroyed.
For 100 years, I will make sure no-one can live there."

There was once a woman named O-sumi. She lived during the Edo Period in what is now Tokushima Prefecture. She moved from the village of Kisawa to the small hamlet of Hose with her three-year-old daughter, O-tama, in order to get married. However, a powerful man by the name of Yahachi fell deeply in love with O-sumi, and that was the beginning of the end.

O-sumi desperately rejected Yahachi's advances, but this just made him angry. Her rejection of him filled Yahachi with rage, and he soon funnelled that hatred into malicious bullying. Yahachi was a powerful and influential man within the small hamlet of Hose, and soon the other villagers began to scorn O-sumi as well. She was ostracised, and with nowhere left to go, pushed to the very edge of her limits.

Holding her young daughter O-tama in her arms, O-sumi stood on the riverbed of the Kaifu River and laid a curse upon the hamlet that had driven her to this point. She carved the words into the wood of a Japanese hackberry tree:

50 years after my death, Hose shall be destroyed. For 100 years, I will make sure no-one can live there.

Why 50 years after her death? Why wait to punish the people that had made O-sumi's life a living hell? Why not punish them immediately and have her sweet, sweet revenge?

Because O-sumi's husband still lived. Despite all that happened, she loved him and wished to give him a chance to escape the terrible fate that would befall the hamlet after her death.

For an hour, O-sumi prayed by the riverbed. Then, she changed O-tama into white clothes and lifted the hoe she had brought with them high into the air. She took aim at her beloved daughter's head and brought the hoe down forcefully, ending her life in an instant. It's said that the blood from her broken head spurted over a metre into the air.

O-sumi filled her mouth with her daughter's blood, and then turned to the heavens and spat it out. She chanted her curse upon Hose over and over.

"Turn Hose into fields, turn it into a heap."

At last she screamed into the mountains with all her might. O-sumi then picked up her daughter, rubbing her cheek to her face and chanting a prayer to the great Buddhist monk Kukai before throwing herself into the river, sealing her curse with her own death…

Destruction of Hose
July 25, 1892
2:00 p.m.

Halfway up Hose Mountain, on the south bank of the Kaifu River, a section roughly 300 metres wide and 800 metres long was destroyed, bringing with it a great sound.

In a lodging on the north bank at the foot of the mountain, 36 people, including those working away from home, and 11 members of the Inoue and Sakurai families were buried alive.

Four hectares of fields were buried, and the hamlet of Hose was wiped out in an instant. This disaster is one the likes of which Tokushima has never before seen in its history.

Just as O-sumi proclaimed, fifty years after her death, Hose was destroyed. Even now, over 100 years later, the mountain Hose was located on is still unfit for human habitation. It's said that if you go to the Kaifu River on the anniversary of O-sumi's death, then you will be able to see two fireballs; one for O-sumi, and one for O-tama, heading towards Hose Mountain before gradually disappearing.

It's uncertain whether O-sumi was a real person, but her legend is enduring. Whether O-sumi actually lived in the hamlet of Hose over 150 years ago, we'll likely never know, but the destruction of Hose Mountain was a very real event.

On July 25, 1892, the mountainside collapsed, taking with it several hectares of fields, completely wiping out the hamlet of Hose, and killing 47 people in a lodging at the bottom of the mountain. This landslide was caused by excessive rains that submerged most of the area and loosened the soil on the mountain, causing one of the biggest disasters in Tokushima's history.

You can find a memorial stone by the side of the road when driving up the mountain today. As you might expect from such a terrible tragedy, it's not just the spirits of O-sumi and her daughter that people claim haunt the mountain, but all of those who lost their lives in the landslide. Memorial stones and towers have been erected to placate the spirits, and one of them details the events that took place that horrific day. It describes how Emperor Meiji heard of the disaster and dispatched some of his most beloved samurai from the eastern part of the country to help the residents get back on their feet.

Fearing the scorned mother's curse, a gravesite was also built for O-sumi and her daughter O-tama on the mountain, now known as the mother and child gravesite. But it appears to have had no effect, as people claim to have experienced supernatural phenomena on the mountain to this day.

Kubikiri Ridge

Location: Prefectural Road 17, Nishibun, Ayagawa, Ayauta District, Kagawa Prefecture, 761-2206

Everybody knew of it. Kubikiri Ridge. The site of a fierce battle between Chosokabe Motochika and the Zoda clan in the Sengoku Era that ended in a massive Zoda defeat. They cut the heads off those who remained, and so the area was called Kubikiri (cutting off heads) Ridge.

Seven university students, bored and looking for a little fun, decided to go visit the area and test their mettle. It was just a story, after all. Something that happened hundreds of years earlier.

They jumped in two cars and headed for the ridge. In contrast to its name, it was a gentle slope, and the drive was peaceful. Trees grew thick by the side of the road, but everything was well maintained and well looked after. It could have been any other highway. There was nothing special about it.

The group decided to get out of the cars and go for a walk. There was no excitement in sitting inside the car and looking at trees. They could do that anywhere. The area looked perfectly safe. As they were walking, they discovered an old path through the dense trees.

The students laughed and joked and entered the path. But as they did, the wind suddenly picked up. The trees rustled loudly around them, like the forest was coming to life.

"Ooooooooooooooooooooooooooo."

A deep, throaty sound rang out around them. It seemed to be coming from everywhere, the sound of a man groaning in pain.

The group ran back to the car at once. The driver started the engine, wanting nothing more than to be as far away from there as possible. But then they noticed one person wasn't in the car yet. He was standing outside, staring at the trees. They dragged him in and sped off.

"You heard that voice, right?"

"It sounded angry."

The person they had to drag into the car turned to them.

"What do you mean? I didn't hear any voice."

The group were confused. They all heard it. Every single one of them. He was the only person claiming to have heard nothing. Why? How could he be the only one?

But the strangeness continued.

When they turned around to see if the second car was following them, they saw the windscreen on the driver's side fogged up. But it wasn't just foggy. It was covered in countless handprints.

What on earth was going on?

The foggy window glass. The innumerable handprints. The guy who claimed he didn't hear a thing. That was when it hit them.

Something was trying to spirit their friend away…

Kubikiri Ridge sits next to Mount Shiro in Kagawa Prefecture. At an elevation of 271 metres, it's not terribly high considering the rest of the mountains around it, and it slopes rather gently. *Kubikiri* means cutting off one's head in Japanese, giving this ghost spot a particularly fitting name.

There are several theories as to how the ridge received its name. Perhaps the most popular is the above-mentioned story of Chosokabe Motochika and his defeat of the Zoda clan during the Sengoku Era. Chosokabe went on to gain control of the entire island of Shikoku during the Warring States Period, and this is said to have been just one of his battles on his way to total victory. In 1579, the clan protecting Zoda Castle were so thoroughly defeated that all those remaining, most of them gravely injured, had their heads cut off on the site of the ridge today. Thus, it came to be known as Kubikiri Ridge. The ridge where heads were cut off.

Another theory suggests that the name came from a peasant uprising in 1726. The peasants were upset with rising taxes and revolted against their masters. But the revolt was unsuccessful. 147 peasants were captured, and of those, 51 were put to death. Their heads were cut off and displayed for all to see, a warning of what would happen if they tried to revolt again. The area became known henceforth as Kubikiri Ridge.

Yet another theory suggests that an even more ancient battle took place between the Miura and Amago clans for control of the local castle. No matter how you look at it, the area has a long and bloody history, and regardless of which theory you believe, it's undeniable that many people have died at the ridge over the years. Often in brutal and humiliating ways.

In 1845, a memorial statue called the Kubikiri Jizo was erected in the area for those who were killed over the years. But rumours of ghostly sightings in the area persist, and night after night, the spirits of those without their heads are said to linger in the trees. If you're unlucky enough to run into one, you might hear something gently whisper into your ear, "Have you seen my head?" Disembodied voices are particularly common, and it's not unheard of to run into a spirit missing one of its limbs, either.

One story tells of a man who was driving up the ridge one night when he saw a man standing in the middle of the road. He stopped his car, thinking it dangerous to go any further. The headlights shone on the man's body, but he couldn't see his head. His clothes look old-fashioned, not something he'd ever seen anyone in the modern period wear before.

Finding the situation more and more strange, he got out of his car and went to approach the man. That was when he realised. He quickly got back into the car, put it into reverse and sped away. The man had no head, and a disembodied voice followed him all the way back down.

Another story tells of a woman who went for a drive with two of her friends. This woman had a strong *reikan*, or ability to sense the supernatural, and as the sun was setting and they were getting ready to return home, one of her friends suggested they stop by Kubikiri Ridge on the way. The woman protested immediately. It was not a safe place to be, and it would be better if they avoided it. But her friend refused to listen, and she drove them there anyway. At the very least, she wanted to get out and have a look at the Kubikiri Jizo statue. She pulled over and got out of the car.

The woman noticed the air felt heavy and oppressive. She tried to stop her friend from going, but she shrugged her off and continued up the path. The woman and her other friend waited, but 30 minutes passed with no sign of their friend. They got out and searched for her for several hours, but they couldn't find her anywhere.

They went to the police and a search party was sent out, but nobody found any sign of her. She was gone. Just like that. The woman suspected that the moment her friend voiced her desire to visit the ridge, it was already too late. The spirits had summoned her there, and they would have what they wanted. Once more she felt that Kubikiri Ridge was a dangerous place. One you shouldn't visit half-hearted.

Shinyuudo Ridge

Location: Prefectural Road 17, Shobu, Matsuyama City, Ehime Prefecture, 799-2412

A young boy was sitting in the back seat as his father drove through Shinyuudo Ridge. He had heard stories from old times that old women were abandoned in the mountain nearby when families were no longer able to look after them. It seemed cruel, but many events of the past were.

They were passing the town of Gishiki when his mother, in the passenger's seat, pointed out the window.

"There's someone out there," she said. The boy looked but couldn't see anyone. Just trees growing up the mountainside.

He didn't think much more of it, but the next day his mother walked into the kitchen looking more worn out than usual.

"I had a strange dream. I was alone in the mountains somewhere, and I couldn't move. I just stared at the trees for hours," she said. When she woke up and looked in the mirror, she saw she looked exhausted. Like she'd aged overnight and become an old woman.

There were bodies in the mountain that people still hadn't found. Bodies of old women who were abandoned by their families and left to die alone, surrounded by nothing but trees. Was that what his mother saw? A vision from an old woman who wanted her body found? An old woman who didn't want to be alone anymore…?

Shinyuudo Ridge sits in the north-west of the island of Shikoku, in Ehime Prefecture. It connects the modern-day cities of Matsuyama City and Imabari City, and leads to the sacred mountain of Mount Takanawa. The name "Shinyuudo" literally means "the road through which one enters death," and there's a very good reason for that name. Mount Takanawa has long been an object of worship, and in the Edo Period came to be known as an *ubasuteyama*, or "mountain where old women are abandoned."

When a family was unable to look after an older relative anymore, they were carried to a mountain such as Takanawa and left there to die in a practice called *ubasute*. These relatives were first carried through the Shinyuudo Ridge to reach the mountain; it was the path one passed through in order to take someone to their death.

The area next to the ridge is known as Gishiki. *Gishiki* in Japanese means "ritual," and it's thought the area received that name because it was the place where families said their last goodbyes, and a ritual was performed for the elderly. These days you can find a large nursing home in the city of Gishiki. What was once an area to abandon old women that a family couldn't take care of is now... an area to abandon old women that a family can't take care of. More about the historical practice of ubasute and Shinyuudo Ridge can also be found in the Ehime history book *Kazahaya District History*.

It's said that the skeletons of the elderly who were abandoned on the sacred mountain of Takanawa are still found regularly, and though their remains have been discovered, their spirits continue to linger around the pass. 10 years ago the name of the ridge was changed from Shinyuudo to Sasaga, perhaps in an attempt to give the ridge a fresh start and a less morbid name. Considering that people continue to claim to see spirits near the ridge to this day, perhaps they weren't that happy with a simple name change.

While the ridge is famous locally for stories of ghosts and abandoned old women, a very real crime took place in 2009 that brought the area nationwide attention.

Nishiyama Yoshie was 21-years-old at the time. She lived in Matsuyama City, and worked at the ticket stand for a ferry company operating between Matsuyama and Hiroshima. Although she quit around the start of the New Year in 2009, her boss described her as possessing "a serious attitude towards her work. But boat-related work is very difficult. She was young and said she wanted a new job."

Nishiyama lived with her younger sister in an apartment in Matsuyama. She was bright, friendly and outgoing, and people were seen coming and going from her apartment all the time. With her good looks and easygoing nature, she was popular with the opposite sex as well.

On January 22, 2009, Nishiyama said goodbye to her younger sister and left their apartment around 6 p.m. It was the last time her sister would ever see her.

On the night of the 23rd, Nishiyama met up with 23-year-old Kawai Ryo, who worked at a senior citizens' home in Iyo City. They met on an online dating site, but an hour and a half after meeting in person, Kawai used his scarf to strangle her to death in his car. He dumped her body on Mount Takanawa, and it wasn't until the next day, around 1 p.m., that a passing couple found her dead body.

Nishiyama was found wearing lightweight clothes, a little odd considering it was the middle of winter. She was barefoot and wearing only jeans and a hooded sweater. The soles of her feet were clean, leading investigators to believe her body had been dumped on the mountainside after her death.

Her hair, usually black, had been dyed light brown, and rather than her usual glasses, she was discovered wearing contacts. Or rather, one contact. It was thought that in the struggle inside Kawai's car that the other fell out. Was she hoping to make a good impression when she met Kawai?

Nobody knows what she did in the 24 hours after leaving her house but before meeting up with her future murderer, but less than two hours after meeting up with him, her corpse was abandoned in the cold winter air halfway up a mountain.

At his trial in July of the same year, Kawai received a 15-year sentence for the murder. He reportedly got angry when he demanded money from Nishiyama and she refused, so he lost his temper and strangled her. The judge remarked that they had met merely an hour and a half before the crime happened, making the crime all the more violent and impulsive. They were simply going for a drive through the mountains when the incident occurred. He then dumped her body close to

Shinyuudo Ridge and fled. But it wasn't until a few weeks later, on February 8, that Kawai was finally arrested for the crime and admitted to the murder.

They say the ghost of Nishiyama still haunts the area near the ridge to this day, along with the spirits of old women who just want their bodies to finally be found all these years later.

KYUSHU

Old Inunaki Tunnel

Location: Inunaki Mountain Pass, Kuyama-cho, Miyawaka-shi, Fukuoka Prefecture, 811-2501

There wasn't a single teenager around who hadn't been there to test their mettle in the deep, dark night. Inunaki Ridge, or perhaps more specifically, Old Inunaki Tunnel. It was closed off and abandoned, but that didn't stop kids from going there to see if the ghost rumours were true or not.

The TV and internet said the area was dangerous. You shouldn't go. But most people who went there went home disappointed. They didn't see the fabled ghosts or anything else out of the ordinary. It was true that violent gangs hung out in the area, so in that sense it was dangerous, but the supernatural? Everyone knew a guy, but no-one had ever seen anything themselves.

The young man was bored. He'd never been to Inunaki Ridge before and decided tonight was going to be the night. He called up some of his friends and they jumped in the car for a late night drive. One of his friends had been there before, but he didn't see anything either. It was a big letdown.

The four young men laughed and chatted as they approached. It was just up ahead. All they had to do was turn at the T-junction.

"Turn left," one of the young man's friends said.

"No, we turned right last time I went," his other friend, the one who had been to Old Inunaki Tunnel before, said.

The young man trusted his friend. He'd actually

been there, after all. There was no reason not to believe him. His other friend sat back and sighed when they turned the other way.

"Pfft. You should have gone over the edge."

His expression scared the three other men in the car. They didn't know what to say.

As expected, they reached the old tunnel by turning right. They found out after that the path to the left had collapsed, leaving a very steep drop. If they had turned that way, they would have driven over the edge and potentially died.

When asked about it, the young man said he had no memory of ever telling them to turn left…

The name "Inunaki" simultaneously brings up images of human brutality and the supernatural within Japan. Located in the north of Kyushu, there have long been rumours of the fabled Inunaki Village, a village hidden deep within the mountains that exists outside the boundaries of the Japanese constitution.

In 2000, a corpse was discovered in the Inunaki Dam, and due to snowfall in the winter, the Inunaki Pass sees numerous traffic accidents each year. The area including the tunnel and surrounding areas is often referred to as the "Inunaki Ridge," but there is one particular incident that stands out above all others. An incident that took place at what is now called the Old Inunaki Tunnel.

The Old Inunaki Tunnel is said to be the greatest ghost spot in all of Kyushu, and one of the great three haunted spots of Japan. One spirit medium even declared the area so dangerous that "Not even those with zero ability to sense the supernatural should go there." Another famous spirit medium, Gibo Aiko, once visited Inunaki Ridge for a television program, but became so ill that she had to cancel recording. Or so they say.

There are several theories as to how the area gained the name "Inunaki," all of which tie in to the eerie atmosphere of Inunaki Ridge and its many supernatural legends. *Inu* means dog and *naki* means cry, so literally the name means "a dog's cry." One legend says the name came from a dog who got lost in the mountains and cried because it was unable to find its way out.

Another says that a hunter went into the mountain with his dog, but the dog wouldn't stop barking so the hunter killed it. When he did, a large snake suddenly appeared. The hunter managed to kill the snake, and then carefully buried his dog in regret.

A third, perhaps more modern reason, suggests that the name comes from the abnormal number of women who get lost in the area. Their cries for help sound like a howling dog, and so the area was named Inunaki.

Work on the Old Inunaki Tunnel began in 1884, but due to the prohibitive costs and lack of engineering knowledge at the time, construction was halted. However, the local village chiefs appealed to prefectural authorities in 1927 for construction to begin anew. The villages banded together, and in 1949 the tunnel was finally opened. The road was narrow and full of sudden curves, however, so with advancements in engineering, a new tunnel was built in 1975 and the old one closed for good.

While the new tunnel measures 1,385 metres in length, it's difficult to tell just how long the old tunnel is now. The plate listing the distance of the old tunnel has rusted over the years, making it illegible, but judging from the air above, people have surmised the old tunnel reaches approximately 150 metres in length.

Thanks to construction on the nearby Inunaki Dam, which started in 1970 and was completed in 1994, two sections of the road leading to the old tunnel were flooded. With the old road no longer in use, people started to use the area for dumping unwanted items, and biker gangs were said to be using the area as a base, so the road and the old tunnel were sealed off. These barricades remain today.

Then, in 1988, a horrific incident took place at Old Inunaki Tunnel that shook the nation. One report of the incident goes as follows:

At midday on December 7, 1988, the burned body of factory worker Umeyama Kouichi (20) was discovered at Inunaki Mountain Pass. Police arrested a group of youths (16~19yo) from the Takawa district under suspicion of killing Umeyama by pouring gasoline on him and setting him on fire.

Umeyama was said to be a very filial young man. At the time of the incident, Umeyama was on his way home from work.

The incident began when the youths approached

Umeyama, who was waiting in his car at a stoplight.

"We need your car to pick up some girls, so quit acting so tough and get out."

When Umeyama refused, the youths attacked and abducted him, where they then assaulted him once more.

Spotting a break in the youths' guard, Umeyama escaped and, despite his injuries, attempted to make his way home. However, unable to get any help from passing cars, he was captured by the group once again.

The angry youths tried to throw Umeyama off Kanda Port, but he clung to the fence with all his might and withstood their assault.

Seeing Umeyama like this, one of the youths felt remorseful, or perhaps fearful, and suggested they should stop. The ringleader, afraid their attack would be discovered, said to his friends, "We're all in this together," and they decided to kill him.

They put Umeyama in the trunk of his car and beat him with cranks, wrenches and other tools. They tried to get rid of the body at Rikimaru Dam, but fearing the body would float, they instead decided to burn it instead so it would be impossible to identify and made for the abandoned Old Inunaki Tunnel.

Arriving at the Old Inunaki Tunnel, they poured gasoline (which they acquired in a PET bottle at a gasoline station on the way, saying their bike had run out of gas) over Umeyama's head. He screamed in terror and it echoed loudly throughout the abandoned tunnel.

Even before the incident, there were many

stories about vengeful ghosts in the old tunnel. Perhaps because of this, the youths flinched for just a moment, and Umeyama took the chance to run again, fleeing into the forest.

The youths called out to him. "We're not gonna do anything, so come out. We're not lying."

Having suffered such violence, it would be hard to believe such a statement, but for some reason Umeyama believed them and made himself known.

The youths captured him for the third time. They stuffed ripped clothes into his mouth, tied his hands and feet, and repeatedly hit him over the head with a stone. It's said the blood spray from this flew far enough to land on the guardrail nearby.

Yet he still wouldn't die, and begging for his life, the youths once again poured gasoline over Umeyama and set him on fire.

Umeyama struggled violently, writhing in pain as he continued asking for help. It's said that burnt remains of his clothes were also found scorched on the guardrail.

Driven mad with pain, Umeyama ran all the way back to the entrance of the tunnel. There, all of his strength finally left his body, and he collapsed.

The youths, wanting to check that Umeyama was actually dead this time, returned to the scene and made sure he was no longer moving before they returned to Fukuoka City.

At a bar afterwards, the youths were heard cheerfully boasting, "We just killed someone! Set him on fire!"

Umeyama's cause of death was said to be blood loss from the head. It's impossible to imagine the pain and suffering he must have been in, his body being set alight until he finally died from loss of blood.

Umeyama's body was discovered at midday the following day, and the youths arrested shortly after.

At the appeal trial held in Fukuoka Court on March 8, 1991, the main perpetrator (21, 19-years-old at the time of the crime, a stallholder helper in Tagawa District, Fukuoka Prefecture), who was handed a sentence of life imprisonment at his first trial, said, "There was no clear intention to kill, the sentence is too harsh," and sought a reduction to his sentence. However, the presiding judge, Maeda Kazuaki, said, "The cruelty displayed is unlike any other seen in similar cases. The defendant played a central role and so bears a heavy responsibility." The appeal was rejected and the other youths also found guilty.

Old Inunaki Tunnel, and the surrounding Inunaki Ridge, is said to be haunted by evil spirits, those with lingering grudges, and those unable to move on, such as the victim in the above incident. Those who visit the area often fall victim to its curse, such as in the following cases.

In 1991, a truck driver accidentally killed his partner at the Inunaki Dam. He then hung himself in penance.

In 1993, a 60-year-old male truck driver rolled his tanker over the side of the road and ended up freezing to death before help could arrive.

In 1996, a married couple threw themselves into the damn on New Year's Day in an apparent suicide pact.

In 2000, a 64-year-old man was kidnapped and later killed. His body was thrown into Inunaki Dam. The culprit received 10 years in prison.

In 2001, four youths were killed "on their way to see ghosts." The driver left home at 3 a.m. and picked up four of his friends. The young men, aged 15 to 18, were on a mission to see ghosts at the Inunaki Ridge. However, on their way back they collided with a truck. The driver and three of his passengers died. Only one boy survived.

The new tunnel isn't free of hauntings either. Various rumours have spread over the years, including those that claim the spirits trapped in the old tunnel has started to move over to the new. Hauntings include:

- A ghostly woman in a white dress seen around the area
- Passengers going mad and requiring hospitalisation
- Cats suddenly going quiet and cowering inside the tunnel
- White shadows banging on the window glass, leaving marks that are near-impossible to erase
- Ghostly limbs that reach out and grab people inside the tunnel
- People disappearing after passing through the tunnel
- Brakes that suddenly stop working inside the tunnel
- The sound of something heavy (like a body)

landing on top of the car, only to find nothing there upon exiting the tunnel
- Voices, footsteps and white shadows chasing cars through the tunnel

Whether ghosts actually haunt the Inunaki Ridge or not, it's undeniable that a large number of horrific incidents have taken place in the area over the last 40 years, and one needs to be especially careful if they feel like ghost hunting in the ridge. It's not an area to take lightly.

Rokkasako Tunnel

Location: 1827-1 Fujikawachi, Usuki City, Oita Prefecture, 875-0084

It was a little before midnight when she was driving home with her husband. They were approaching Rokkasako Tunnel, a creepy, little-used tunnel by that point. Her husband seemed nervous. He was looking around and shifting constantly in his seat.

"Is everything okay?" she asked, squeezing his hand. He squeezed back even tighter, and then suddenly let go and pushed the rear-view mirror up so they couldn't see it.

"What's wrong?" his wife asked. He shook his head, his complexion turning pale.

"I saw a woman. She was with a small child. I've seen them three times now, but…"

The wife hadn't seen anyone. The roads were empty, and she most certainly wouldn't have missed a woman and child standing by the side. Three times, no less.

But now that he mentioned it, while she couldn't see anyone herself, she could feel something. What did they call it? A sixth sense. It was like someone was watching them not too far in the distance.

"Shit, the road's out."

Her husband pointed to a sign before Rokkasako Tunnel. There were fallen rocks and it was dangerous to pass through, but the tunnel wasn't blocked.

"Let's just go through. It's not that long."

But the wife's senses were on fire. She knew that

if they went inside, they would see that woman and child for a fourth, and perhaps final, time.

"No. Let's turn around and find another way home."

Something was watching them from nearby. Something wanted them to go in…

Deep in the mountains of Oita Prefecture, in the northern part of Kyushu, there lies an old tunnel. They say that if you visit this tunnel, four days later you will fall victim to sleep paralysis. As you lay frozen in your bed, unable to move a muscle, suddenly you will hear the voice of a small child out of nowhere. But what does the child want…?

Rokkasako Tunnel sits roughly 600 metres from Oita Prefectural Road Route 205, a general road connecting Usuki City with Sakanoichi. When Route 205 was a toll road, people often took a detour through the mountains and Rokkasako Tunnel to avoid paying fees. However, once Route 205 dropped the tolls and became free to use, almost all traffic through Rokkasako ceased. Unlike most tunnels that eventually become ghost spots, Rokkasako is still technically in use; it's just so out of the way and doesn't go anywhere that the larger and more convenient Route 205 can't take you that no-one has any need to use it anymore.

A few hundred metres away you can find the Rokkasako Hot Spring, the only business in the area. It was said that during the Gembun Era (1736-1740) an injured heron flew down and dipped its leg into a pool of water lying in the rice fields. It was miraculously healed, and the area became a well-known hot spring attraction. The hot spring is well-loved by locals, and people have been known to come from all over Japan to stay a night and bath in its healing waters. The name Rokkasako itself is said to have come from the name Rokugasako, the area's old name which used the Chinese characters to describe the coming of the heron.

But with such a peaceful, even soothing history to the area, how did Rokkasako Tunnel become a ghost spot?

Rokkasako is roughly 170 metres long and was carved out of the mountains. Nobody knows when the tunnel was finished; there's no nameplate detailing the tunnel's construction details. The inside certainly lends to its haunted reputation. It is an unlined tunnel, a common method for constructing tunnels in Japan's past. Tunnels were often carved through the mountainside without any steel or supports to keep them raised.

The walls of Rokkasako are rough and uneven bare rock, like that of a cave, and are constantly leaking water. You can even find stalactites forming on the roof. The tunnel is tucked into the mountains in the middle of nowhere, surrounded by nothing but forests and old abandoned houses lining the road. The perfect location for some ghost stories to spring to life.

Rokkasako is one of those tunnels that became a ghost spot not due to any real-life incidents, but thanks to how creepy-looking it is. It's dark, even during the middle of the day. The walls are made of bare, uneven rock that constantly leaks water. And while it's not abandoned, it might as well be for how little traffic it sees. Once Route 205 became the main thoroughfare in the area, it didn't take long for rumours to start about the now-unnecessary Rokkasako Tunnel.

If you ask any ghost hunter worth their salt what's haunting Rokkasako these days, they will inevitably answer that it's haunted by the ghosts of a woman and child. They say that if you drive through the tunnel, you will see a woman standing by the side of the road, but when you look in the rear-view or side mirrors, she will be gone. Other people claim that when you drive through the tunnel, a child's handprint will appear on the window glass.

But who are the woman and child? Are they related? Did they die in an accident inside the tunnel? Or were they murdered nearby? There are rumours that a skeleton was found in the woods near the tunnel, but much like the rumours of the ghosts themselves, no solid evidence exists of such an event ever happening. But who ever let lack of evidence get in the way of a good story?

As you might expect, Rokkasako Tunnel makes a great *kimodameshi* spot. One ghost hunter who visited the tunnel told of a university friend who, 10 years earlier, visited the tunnel with a group of friends to test their courage. They dropped two people off at one end of the tunnel, then dropped another two off at the other end. They met in the middle and then returned together. Nothing happened to the group inside the tunnel, but on the way home, one of the group claimed to feel sick, and the next day fell ill to a fever that lasted five days. According to the ghost hunter's friend, "He brought that woman back with him…"

Rokkasako Tunnel is a prime example of Japan's ability to take any old creepy place and give it new life as a ghost spot… whether anything actually happened there or not. After all, there are a lot of ghost hunters around Japan who love to travel the country looking for new scares to update their blogs with. A little ghostly tourism does a countryside town good.

Kaimon Tunnel

Location: 6743 Kaimonkawashiri, Ibusuki City, Kagoshima Prefecture, 891-0602

At the foot of Kaimondake Volcano, there's a tunnel. Technically, it's two tunnels, but it was built in the 1960s to take people around the volcano. Word was, it was also haunted.

Unlike most haunted tunnels, the Kaimon Tunnel was still in use. It was the only way around the volcano by car. One night, a man and his girlfriend decided to go for a drive. Maybe they might get lucky and see one of the fabled ghosts.

There was a rumour of a woman who peeked in from the open spaces in the roof. The tunnel had no lights, so at regular intervals there were spaces cut into the roof to let natural light in. It was said a woman killed herself nearby, and she spent her time after death looking down from the tunnel roof. If you locked eyes with her, it meant you would have an accident on your way home.

They drove through the dark tunnel, the only light coming from the car's headlights. The tunnel was narrow; so narrow that only one car could fit through at a time. It was also long. Incredibly long. It felt like they were driving forever. The driver looked up at the roof, but he saw nothing. No woman looking down. Either he was lucky, or it really was just a rumour.

Then the car stalled. It was an automatic. There was no reason for it to suddenly stall. The man tried over and over to get it going again, but nothing was working. His girlfriend turned and looked out the back window. Suddenly her face changed and her expression dropped. All the colour drained from her cheeks. It was like she'd seen a ghost.

"Something's coming!"

The pair started to panic. The man couldn't see anything, but his girlfriend's screaming and shaking were enough to let him know that they needed to get out of there, and soon.

He turned the key, over and over. The engine roared to life as his girlfriend grabbed his arm and yanked on his sleeve. They sped out of the tunnel, and when they were safely outside, the man's girlfriend pointed to her ankle, her arm trembling. There was a handprint, bright and angry staring back at them.

The pair went to the closest shrine they could find and asked the priest to purify them. They agreed never to drive through that tunnel again…

Kaimon Tunnel sits at the foot of Kaimon Volcano, a volcano that rises 900 metres into the air and is one of the southernmost points of Japan. It's also where it gets its name, although that's not its official one, nor is it technically one tunnel. Its official name is "Okuramoto Tunnel No. 1" (the southern part) and "Okuramoto Tunnel No. 2" (the northern part). But most people call it by its common name of Kaimon Tunnel.

The tunnel is extremely narrow. Only one car can fit through at any time, and in parts it's impossible to even open the car door. There are a few waiting sections inbuilt just in case two cars happen to be in the tunnel at the same time, but they are few and far between.

The open area between the tunnels is covered by a wire skeleton, so it's likely the tunnel was meant to be continuous, but for some reason, only that part remains unfinished.

The southern part of the tunnel is 152 metres long, while the northern part is 625 metres long. There is no electric lighting, so holes were cut into the tunnel roof at regular intervals to let natural light in. This makes it, at best, gloomy during the day, and at worst, pitch black at night.

It might seem like every tunnel in Kyushu is haunted, but unlike most, Kaimon Tunnel is still in use. It's not abandoned nor has it been cordoned off. You can drive through it today and investigate for yourself whether it really is haunted or not. But beware, because there are a lot of stories about it.

There were once rumours that a field hospital was built at the foot of the volcano during the Second World War, but no evidence has ever been found that this was true. Many troops were stationed in the area when Japan feared American invasion, but there was never a field hospital and it never saw battle. More recent rumours suggest the area is a popular suicide spot, with its wealth of dense forest and rocky beaches nearby.

One woman supposedly hung herself in the area, and her spirit now haunts the tunnel from above, peeking in through the holes in the tunnel roof. If you're unlucky enough to see her looking down at you as you drive by, prepare yourself. That means you can expect to have an accident on your way home.

Several drivers have reported finding their rear seat drenched in water after passing through the tunnel. As you may recall from Aoyama Cemetery and the legend of the ghost in the taxi, this is a fairly common occurrence with Japanese spirits. The spirits have an intense connection to water, and with rumours of suicides on the beach nearby, it's not too difficult to see how this rumour began here as well.

And like the couple in the opening tale, there are rumours that spirits will chase cars inside the tunnel at night, and if they catch you, they will leave their mark. This may or may not require a visit to a nearby shrine for purification, but when it comes to Japanese ghosts, it's better to be safe than sorry.

There's another potential reason for why ghosts haunt this particular tunnel. A local legend that has been around since the tunnel was first completed.

At the bottom of Kaimon Volcano, and to the north of the tunnel, is a golf course. When that golf course was first under construction, it was plagued by accidents. The workers complained that it was a curse; they were angering the spirits, and they were taking their revenge upon them. The workers went to be purified at a local shrine, but it did nothing. The accidents continued.

The man in charge, trying to find out what was going on, went to speak with some locals.

"There's an important shrine near here called Hirakiki Shrine," they told him. "They worship the god of the sea there, and the spirits of those who die in shipwrecks find their way back to that shrine.

The path they take back passes through Kaimon Volcano, so the golf course you're building is in their way."

They were unable to stop construction of the golf course after so much work had already been done. So the leader came up with a new idea. A new type of construction unseen in Japan at the time. He would build a Spirit Path. Give the spirits a new way to reach the shrine.

But that would cost money, and they would have to officially add it to the budget. So they came up with a plan. To the general public, it would be known as a general throughway. An easy and safe way to travel around the volcano. They built the tunnel, and after that, the accidents stopped. Construction went smoothly and the golf course was finished.

If you believe the stories, Kaimon Tunnel continues to lead spirits to Hirakiki Shrine to this day, directing them away from the golf course. But not all pass through it completely. Some linger, it is said, and continue to haunt the living who pass through instead.

Oyama Kaizuka

Location: Ooyama 2 Chome 12-1, Ginowan City, Okinawa Prefecture, 901-2223

As a young boy, he grew up just down the road from Oyama Kaizuka, a famous spiritual training ground for Okinawa's infamous shamans, the *yuta*. Half doctors, half shamans. That's how the populace thought of them. Ever since he could remember, his parents always told him, "You must never go there. It's too dangerous."

But then one day, a family from the north of the island moved in two houses down. They also had a son the same age, and he was a rather rambunctious child. The two boys quickly became friends, and they ran around town with their own little gang, getting up to mischief.

One day, as the sun was setting, the neighbour's boy suggested they head over to the yuta training ground. Someone had been training there recently, and their cries were getting wilder and more terrifying as the nights went on. Whatever that yuta was facing, they seemed to be struggling with it.

"It's a curse," the young boy's parents said. He had no idea what went on in Oyama Kaizuka when the yuta trained there. He didn't know that the yuta invited evil spirits in, and then worked hard to exorcise them again. Little by little, they invited even stronger spirits, training their powers like a bodybuilder trains their muscles.

But if a yuta was lacking in skill, those spirits would eat away at them, bit by bit, until finally escaping into the wild.

The yuta they heard screaming night after night was a woman.

All the boys' gang agreed. If the yuta was in trouble, then they should help her. They entered the back path through the trees. Trees so dense it was like a thick forest. The concrete path turned into gravel, but they pressed forth. The boy's heart beat wildly in his chest. His legs shook with each scream that pierced the night.

Finally, they found the woman. She really was a yuta, and it really was a yuta training ground after all. They weren't just wild rumours.

She groaned, her voice raw and harsh. Black coils of something the boy didn't understand seemed to float in the air around her.

The neighbours' boy had no plan, but he stepped forward and approached the woman. She saw him coming and turned to look at him. Her eyes were possessed; black and bloodshot. Her face was pale blue. She looked just like the spirits she was supposed to be fighting.

She ran at the boys, screaming and groaning. The boys panicked. An unknown creature was running right for them. They fled in different directions, screaming in terror, eventually making their way back to the public hall.

But one of the boys was missing. They looked everywhere for him, but he was nowhere to be seen. Did the yuta get him? Or perhaps whatever spirit was possessing the yuta? Did he get lost in the trees? Why wasn't he back yet?

Then they saw him. He came limping towards

them, the skin on his knees scraped off. He just fell over while escaping, he said. That was all. But the boys didn't care. They were just glad he was safe.

But 10 minutes later, they noticed a change in him. Dark bags were growing under his eyes which stared out blankly before him. Drool dribbled down his chin. He groaned and then fell over.

They called an ambulance, but the boy remained unconscious.

Half doctor, half shaman. That's what the boy's parents said. His friend needed help. Help that only a shaman could give. He told them about what happened and begged for them to find a skilled yuta to help his friend.

The boy was possessed by 59 different spirits. The spirits of those summoned to the yuta training grounds. It was a miracle they were able to save him, but save him they did.

The boy had no memory of what happened in the time he was missing. One moment he was running from the female yuta, and the next he was in front of the public hall with his friends. But there was one thing they were certain of. After that night, nobody heard the cries of the female yuta again…

Oyama Kaizuka is an important place of cultural heritage in Okinawa. It's also said to be one of the most haunted spots in Japan. Located about 700 metres from the Ginowan Seaside Park, Oyama Kaizuka has long been an important religious and burial site for the people of Okinawa.

It sits deep in the forest, and can be identified by a small shrine that sits before a cave. That cave was used as an air-raid shelter during the Second World War, and so people in modern times have grown to fear it. Past the shrine is said to be the "land of the dead," and those who enter may never return. Even the local council has to constantly remind people not to enter, a rarity for ghost spots around Japan.

Oyama Kaizuka, which translates directly as "large mountain shell heap," is these days said to be a training ground for Okinawan spirit mediums known as yuta. Yuta are mediums born with particularly strong spiritual powers, and Oyama Kaizuka is sacred land to them. Because the spirits are so strong there, they can hone their natural abilities and make them stronger, much like a martial artist trains his body for a fight.

The area is also famous because the caves were used as an air-raid shelter during the Second World War. Upon hearing Japan lost the war, the people taking refuge killed themselves, fearing the American soldiers would kill them anyway. This, combined with the fact that yuta trained there, makes Oyama Kaizuka the perfect location for ghost tales and creepy legends.

It's said to be dangerous for anyone with spiritual abilities to enter the grounds because of the strength of the spirits there. There's a sign placed before the grounds that says, "Past this point is sacred land, so please do not play here." The locals also make a point not to go near it at night.

People who do make the mistake of entering the sacred grounds are said to hear an excruciating ringing in their ears, experience sleep paralysis, and also face potential injury upon returning home.

One story tells of four men who used the caves as a place to find shelter from the rain. However, as the rain finally let up and the men tried to leave, one man was grabbed by the legs and dragged back into the cave. His companions fled and the next day he was found dead. The incident made local newspapers.

It's also said that those who visit Oyama Kaizuka by car will find they have troubles on their way home. This can include lights not working, radios suffering from interference, and other mechanical problems. Those who take photos or record video footage at the shrine and cave may often find they've captured the ghosts of children on film, and you can find several of these home videos on the internet today.

Another story tells of a foreign couple who moved to the area and were unaware of the significance of Oyama Kaizuka. They took pictures of the shrine, and when they developed them several days later, they found a white shadow shaped like a katana, and several white glowing orbs in the pictures. When they asked the locals about it, they told the couple the truth of the area, and the couple grew fearful. Yet nothing bad happened to them, and the villagers told them that the local gods must have been welcoming them instead.

The sacred site once featured on an episode of *Getsuyou Kara Yoru Fukashi*. The program interviewed several locals who all agreed the area was terribly dangerous, and it was well known that anyone who visited the area would find themselves sick or injured once they returned home. The power of the spirits that haunt Oyama Kaizuka are said to be so strong that even simply investigating the area can cause the researcher to fall ill... I'll have to get back to you on that one.

There is no denying that Oyama Kaizuka has important cultural significance to the people of Okinawa. It's generally not recommended that people enter dark caves unassisted either, and considering its horrific history, it's not too difficult to see why Oyama Kaizuka is one of the most famous ghost spots in Okinawa, the only part of Japan directly touched by the Second World War.

Chibichiri Gama Cave

Location: 1153 Namihira, Yomitan, Nakagami District, Okinawa Prefecture, 904-0322

She was 22-years-old and bored out of her mind. She lived in Okinawa, the land of beaches and eternal sunshine. Surely there was something to do? She jumped in the car with three of her friends and they decided to go for a late night drive. It was better than sitting at home, and maybe they'd find something to kill their boredom.

It was around midnight when they decided they should go home. But then one of her friends suggested they stop by a famous ghost spot instead. That ghost spot was Chibichiri Gama Cave. It was used as an air-raid shelter during the Second World War, and numerous people had lost their lives there. Everyone agreed, and off they went.

Wide-open dark fields opened up around them as they approached. The cave was only 600 metres from the beach, but it was surrounded by rice fields. In the dark of night, with nobody around, the place was creepy. Too creepy. They got out to have a quick look around, but soon decided to go home. There was something about the place. It felt wrong. It felt off.

They stopped by a nearby convenience store to buy some drinks. The woman turned around to look at the car and, in the overhead lights, saw what looked to be a child's handprints all over the driver's side windscreen.

It was her friend's car. She asked if she knew of

any children that were near it lately, but she couldn't think of any. Not only that, they'd been driving around for hours, and the car was rather dirty. The handprints were recent. Very recent.

A few days later, another of their friends had an accident and broke her leg. It didn't take a genius to figure out what was going on. They went somewhere they shouldn't have. And now they were paying for it...

On April 1, 1945, American soldiers invaded Okinawa at Yomitan Village. Ever since the year before, the Okinawans had been using the nearby caves to take shelter during bombardments, and on this day, the locals ran to the Chibichiri Gama Cave, roughly 600 metres from the beach. In the Okinawan dialect, *chibichiri* means something that has an abrupt ending. There was a small river in the valley that flowed through the cave, but nobody knew where it went. It just seemed to end suddenly, and thus, the cave was named Chibichiri. *Gama* means cave in the same dialect.

Villagers gathered in the caves each day as their homes were bombarded from above. They would take shelter from 8 a.m. and not come out until 5 p.m. each day. But at 9 a.m. on April 1, the American soldiers landed on the beach and made their way towards the cave.

The headquarters of the civil defence unit was located 600 metres away, in Shimuku Gama Cave; another cave connected to Chibichiri. The leader was a former soldier, and the majority of the members were 13 to 15-year-old boys.

"Come out!" the American soldiers called to the villagers inside the cave. But they had been told about the evils of the American and British soldiers, and panic began to set in. An 18-year-old girl attempted to calm everyone inside. "We don't have to fear the Americans. Fight them with your spears." Everyone had with them spears made of bamboo, and at her words, a calm settled over the cave once more.

The villagers initially thought the Americans had parachuted in; if that was so, there wouldn't be many of them, so they would be able to take them out with their spears. They had no idea the army had arrived via the beach, and when the first villagers ran out of the cave screaming bloody murder, they were mowed down by machine gun fire and grenades. Their spears, only two metres in length, were far too short to reach the top of the cliff the Americans were firing from.

The Americans eventually stopped firing and tried to lure the villagers back out with flyers, food, and tobacco. But the villagers refused to believe what was written on the flyers, and no-one touched the food. The former Japanese soldier piled up the futons in the cave and set fire to them, hoping to commit suicide. But one girl threw herself on the pile before the fire could take and put it out.

By the time the next day rolled around, the villagers were stuck in a cramped cave with little ventilation and less oxygen. The American soldiers returned at 8 a.m. and called to the villagers to come out peacefully. But the former Japanese soldier proclaimed that if anyone left, they would be killed, and no-one made a move.

"Kill me," a young girl begged her mother. The villagers had no hope left. The barbaric Americans were waiting for them on the surface, and they had no food and very little oxygen left. They had no choice. It was death by the Americans, or death by their own hands. The mother took a knife and drew it across her own daughter's neck. She then did the same for her son before taking her own life.

The former soldier once again lit the futons, and this time the cave filled with smoke. But those who preferred a quick death on the surface ran out of the cave. To their surprise, they were not killed. Instead, they were sent to Toya in Kyushu for asylum.

139 people were stuffed inside the Chibichiri Gama Cave. Of those, 82 committed suicide rather than face the American firing squad (according to some reports, that number was actually as high as 85). The majority of people who died in the cave were children under the age of 18.

In 1987, a statue was erected in memory of those who lost their lives at the cave during the war. In November of that same year, it was destroyed, and it wasn't until 1995 that the statue was rebuilt. The area also became off-limits due to requests of the families of the deceased. It was a gravesite, not a place to be playing around in.

But in September 2017, once again the memorial statue was destroyed, and the cave was discovered in a state of disarray. The paper cranes left by junior high students were ripped apart, the vases inside were broken, and even the ashes of the dead were strewn around the cave floor.

Four local teenagers were arrested for the crime; a crime the mayor described as "unthinkable for anyone with common sense." The boys' motive for the crime was *kimodameshi*. A test of courage. They were released on probation, and made to clean up the cave, apologise to the families of the deceased, and write a report about the mass suicide that took place during the war.

According to spirit mediums who have visited the cave, the air is heavy during the day, and at night, the sounds of voices can still be heard crying throughout. It's not a place one should visit for kimodameshi, and not just because of common sense. The spirits of those killed during the war are said to linger, and it is rude to disrespect the dead.

SOURCES

The following is a list of websites visited while gathering information for this book.

2Channel: https://2ch.live/
2NN: https://www.2nn.jp/
Anabre: https://anabre.net/
Aoki Sazae Ten: http://aokisazae.eshizuoka.jp/
Ashura: http://www.asyura2.com/
Aviation Safety Network: http://aviation-safety.net/
Bakusai: http://bakusai.com/
Believe It Or Not: https://believeitornot666.com/
Bizamurai: https://bizamurai.com/
Career Develop: http://yuekijyoho.net/
Dai Nippon Kanko Shinbun: https://bjtp.tokyo/
Date Spot: http://datespo.jp/
Fushigi Net: http://world-fusigi.net/
Chiiki no Jikenbo: http://tiiki-no-jikenbo.com/
Ghost Map: https://ghostmap.net/
Gibo Kantei: http://www.gibo-kantei.com/
Haikyo Kensaku Chizu: https://haikyo.info/
Hajimete Mama: https://hajimetemama.com/
Hiroshima Kankou Nabi: https://www.hiroshima-kankou.com/
Honkowa Toshi Densetsu: https://honkowanet.com/
Honogurai Osanpo: http://honoguraiosanpo.blog.jp/
Honto ni Atta Kowai Hanashi: https://kowai.osusumen.jp/
Honto ni Kowakatta Shinrei Spot Taikendan: https://stories-of-scary-spiritspot.com/
Horror Researcher Hiroyuki no Occult Zatsudan Blog: https://ameblo.jp/hiroaroma/
Hoshi no Machi Katano Blog: http://murata35.chicappa.jp/
HuffPost: https://www.huffingtonpost.jp/

I Love Hokkaido: https://blogs.yahoo.co.jp/tankentai1202/
Icotto: https://icotto.jp/
Ierabu: https://www.ielove.co.jp/
Iwale: http://iwale.net/
J-Cast News: https://www.j-cast.com/
Jalan: https://www.jalan.net/
Jitsuroku! Honto ni Atta Kowai Hanashi: https://blogs.yahoo.co.jp/to7002/
Keroyume: https://keroyume.exblog.jp/
Kiki Times: http://kikitimes.com/
Kimagure Family: https://kimagurefamily.com/
Kitohan: http://www.kitohan.sakuraweb.com/
Kowabana: http://kowabana.jp/
Kowai Hanashi ga Kikeru: http://www.kowaiohanasi.info/
Kowai Hanashi, Toshi Densetsu Daisuki na Hito: https://abcd08.biz/
Kyofu no Izumi: https://xn--u9jv84l7ea468b.com/
Kyojin Nikki: https://blog.goo.ne.jp/mixi_goo_1969/
Live For The Moment: https://blogs.yahoo.co.jp/hhhwwe000/
Livedoor News: http://news.livedoor.com/
Lifehack Analyzer: https://lifehack-analyzer.com/
Loyal Hero's Haikyo: http://hhheellhammer666.blogspot.com/
Matome Matome: https://matomame.jp/
Michi Naru Basho o Motomete: https://deth.exblog.jp/
Miyazaki Tsutomu Jiken Enzai Setsu: http://std2g.web.fc2.com/
MSN Atlas: https://mnsatlas.com/
My Navi News: https://news.mynavi.jp/
Naver Matome: https://matome.naver.jp/
Nihon Chin Spot Hyakkei: https://bqspot.com/
Nikutaiha Writer: http://yukinari1204.hatenablog.com/
Nippon no Tabi: https://hirotravel.com/

Nippon Ryokoki: https://tabi-and-everyday.com/
Nippon Sumizumi Kanko: http://nippon-sumizumi-kanko.com/
Noroi Kenkyu Majutsu Jissen: http://noroi.xyz/
Occult Chronicle: https://okakuro.org/
Oshii Hiroshima Jaken!: http://carrotstudio.net/
Ouji no Kitsune: https://blog.goo.ne.jp/kitsunekonkon/
Power Spot Search: http://powerspot-search.info/
Ranpo: https://ranpo.co/
Reiji Ueda: https://ameblo.jp/reiziueda/
Roji Ura: http://www.roji-ura.com/
Ryusuido: http://www.ryusuidou.com/
Sanin Department Store: https://ameblo.jp/sanin-department-store/
Sapporo Minamiku Matome Log: http://matometai.blog.jp/
Scary: http://scary.jp/
Sekai no Fushigi na Monogatari: http://ranblog.info/
Shinrei Channel: http://shinrei.ldblog.jp/
Shinrei Douga: http://shinreydouga.info/
Shinrei Report: http://blog.livedoor.jp/msinnreim/
Shinrei Spot (Ifu): https://haunted-place.info/
Shinrei Spot Kyofu Taikendan: https://shinrei-spot.info/
Shiribeshian: https://blogs.yahoo.co.jp/kony4194/
Shiro Log: http://shirolog.net/
Shoboon News: http://entamenews777.com/
Sore Yuke: https://ameblo.jp/moon-at-noon39/
Syasin.biz: https://syasin.biz/
Takuo no Blog: https://tktktakunet.com/
Tansaku Hiyori: https://tansakunoato.blog.fc2.com/
Tantei File: http://www.tanteifile.com/
Team Kokudo: http://www.geocities.jp/teamkokudo/
The Choice Is Yours: https://pinonon.com/
The Occult Site: http://occult.xxxblog.jp/
Tocana: https://tocana.jp/
Tokyo Deep: https://tokyodeep.info/

Toshi Densetsu! Geinokai no Yami: http://www.airly.net/
Toshi Densetsu ~Kokontozai~: http://sfushigi.com/
Toshi Densetsu Kowai Hanashi: http://toshidj.blog.fc2.com/
Tokyo Park Association: https://www.tokyo-park.or.jp/
Travel Star: https://travel-star.jp/
Trend Wakuwaku Sokuho: http://trend-777.seesaa.net/
Unsolved: http://www.geocities.jp/bowel_of_beelzebub/
Wikipedia: https://ja.wikipedia.org/
Yahoo! Japan Chiebukuro: https://detail.chiebukuro.yahoo.co.jp/
Yamayama Saihakken: http://blog.livedoor.jp/jump8080/
Yurei Spot: http://yuurei.xxxblog.jp/
Zenkoku Kaiki Genshou File: http://shinreispot.com/
Zottosuru Kowai Hanashi: http://kowainakowaina.blog.fc2.com/

WANT EVEN MORE JAPANESE HORROR?

Read a sample from *Toshiden: Exploring Japanese Urban Legends*, also by Tara A. Devlin.

Sugisawa Village

Hidden deep within the mountains of Aomori Prefecture there exists a village called Sugisawa. One day a man from the village went crazy. Within a single day he killed everyone living in the village and then took his own life.

Nobody knows why he went crazy, nor why he went on such a violent crime spree. But the end result of this horrific crime remained the same: Sugisawa Village became empty.

The events of that day were so cruel that the local government decided to leave the village abandoned, and at the same time deny anything ever took place. They then erased all trace of the village from the local maps.

Luckily the village was deep in the mountains, so it was easy to cover the events up. But, of course, they couldn't erase the fact that the horrific crime *did* take place in the first place.

There were rumours of thick bloodstains all over the village, and those who approached the village would undoubtedly be cursed by the evil spirits that lived there.

Furthermore, according to the legend, it's

impossible to reach Sugisawa unless you leave the straight path that leads further into the mountains. Then you will find a sign with a warning standing at the entrance. That sign states, "You may enter, but do so at your own risk."

You can also find an old red shrine gate at the entrance, and a stone shaped like a skull sitting at its feet.

ABOUT

The legend of Sugisawa Village first appeared in the 1990s, although the events mentioned in the legend itself are purported to take place early in the Showa era (the late 1920s and early 30s). The story was one of the first and biggest to be spread through the internet in a time when it was just starting to take off. The story became so popular that several media outlets picked up on it, and it was through the TV show *Kiseki Taiken Unbelievable* in 2000 that it truly reached the masses. The episode set out to find this fabled village and determine whether it actually existed or not. They searched throughout not just Aomori Prefecture but similar stories all over Japan, but in the end they never found it. The program then claimed that Sugisawa Village must exist in a space-time warp, able to appear and disappear at will. After the program aired many people set out to find the village themselves, uploading blog entries and later YouTube videos on their findings, many of which you can still watch on the internet today. Despite claims to the contrary, nobody has ever found the 'real' Sugisawa Village of legend, and it's unlikely anyone ever will.

HISTORY

The legend of Sugisawa Village began in Aomori, the place the village is supposed to be located. There was a real village call Kosugi. It was a small village in the Obatakezawa district of Aomori City. This area received its name because of "a mountain stream that flows through the cedar forest." *Sugi* means cedar and *sawa* means marsh or mountain stream. People would say they were going to 'the cedar,' which sounded a lot like the word 'Sugisawa' in Japanese, and thus it came to be affectionately called that. However, the village was only accessible by foot, and as the years passed it became abandoned because of depopulation, not a murderous crime spree. So how did the benign village of Sugisawa become the fabled site of such a horrific crime?

There was an actual crime in 1938, the same time the Sugisawa legend is supposed to have happened, that took place in the small village of Kamo, close to Tsuyama in Okayama Prefecture. A man, Mutsuo Toi (21 at the time) killed 30 people and injured three before killing himself. Toi had tuberculosis, and in his suicide note claimed that the villagers treated him cruelly, so he wished to extract revenge. He snuck into people's homes over the course of a single night and using a shotgun, katana and axe killed over half the village's occupants, before killing himself at dawn. Although Okayama and Aomori are separated by quite a distance, somehow the story of this crime in Okayama was adapted to the abandoned village in Aomori and became the modern day legend of Sugisawa Village.

There exist even more crazy rumours about the truth of Sugisawa. Some claim it's actually a cover-up for a secret government Echelon base, while others have claimed it's a settlement for old Templar Knights. Apparently you can find Jesus Christ's grave in Aomori Prefecture as well. Who knew?

FINDING THE VILLAGE

There are several key signs that you have stumbled upon Sugisawa Village:

1. There is a sign at the entrance that states, "You must not proceed past this point. There can be no guarantee for your life if you do." There are variations on the exact wording, but in every version the sign states that if you go past it, you will be in big trouble.
2. There is an old, red shrine gate at the entrance to the village, beneath which you'll find a stone that's shaped like a skull.
3. Upon entering the village you'll find several abandoned buildings with bloodstains on the walls.

WITNESS'S ACCOUNTS

There are several creepypastas on the internet from

people who claim to have visited Sugisawa. The following is a common tale shared amongst friends of friends:

One day, two young men and a woman went for a drive deep in the mountains when they got lost and stumbled upon an old, beat up shrine gate. Beneath the gate there were two large stones, one of them shaped like a skull.

The young driver saw it and remembered a rumour he'd heard long ago. The rumour was that a skull found at the bottom of a shrine gate was a sign of the entrance to Sugisawa.

The two men got out of the car; however, the young woman said to them, "I'm scared, let's get out of here." They decided to search the village, however, and all went in together.

About 100 metres after passing under the shrine gate they suddenly found a large open area before them with four old, abandoned buildings. The three of them stepped inside one of the buildings and inside they found a large amount of dried blood on the walls.

The two men felt a shiver run up their spines, and the woman suddenly cried out.

"Hey, there's something strange about this place. I can feel a presence!"

The three of them fled the building in surprise, and as they did, they felt like they were being surrounded by a large number of people.

The three of them ran for the car. However, something was wrong. No matter how much they ran they couldn't seem to reach the car.

The open space to the car should have only been 100 metres, and it was a straight path so there's no way they could have gotten lost. Even so, as the three of them kept running and running they couldn't escape from Sugisawa.

Unawares, the woman suddenly found herself separated from the two men, and as she kept running for what felt like forever she somehow finally found herself back at the car. Thankfully, the keys were still in the ignition. She climbed into the driver's seat to go and get help and turned the key to start the car.

However, no matter how much she turned the key the car refused to start. On the verge of tears she kept turning the key, over and over, trying to get the car to go.

Then…

Don don don.

A large sound suddenly reverberated from the windscreen. She looked and noticed the windscreen was covered in bloody red handprints.

No, not just the windscreen. Countless bloody red handprints appeared on all the windows as though they were all being beat upon at the same time.

The woman crouched down in fear, and before long she fainted…

The next morning one of the locals, out for a morning walk, stumbled upon the bloody car and the dumbfounded young woman inside. Her hair had turned white from fear overnight.

She was taken to the hospital where she explained her terrifying experience. Afterwards she disappeared and was never seen again. Her two male friends were also never found.

The following is a tale from someone calling themselves Matsu-san:

This is a story someone who went to Sugisawa Village told me. They were driving up the mountain when they finally found a gravel road they could pass through when they found a sign. They ignored it and kept going before they realised they'd arrived at Sugisawa Village. The place apparently stank of garbage.

There were a few wooden buildings and a lot of rubbish lying around. This person felt someone watching them, though, and feeling creeped out they left. A few days later a friend who was with the person at the time died.

And the following is from Keiko-san in Saitama:

I went to Aomori Prefecture to go mountain climbing. About two hours into climbing the area was wrapped in fog, and I couldn't see well. I made my way slowly up the mountain so I didn't fall and there were several villages along the way.

Then it was like there was this village smack bang in the middle of the jungle. It was dark, so I pulled out my torch and approached it. There were six buildings in total, and I went from house to house checking each one. There was no sign that anybody lived there. All I saw were two cats.

While I was walking around, I sensed somebody

approaching me, yet when I looked around nobody was there. It was incredibly strange.

There were houses further back in the village as well, but I was too scared to go and look at them. About 20 minutes later I noticed a man standing behind me. He was wearing a straw hat and had pale skin and blue eyes. I said hello, but he said nothing in reply. I paid him no attention and kept walking, but then he suddenly screamed and ran at me.

I ran and finally reached the sign that stated I was back on the mountain climbing track. That was the first time I'd ever been so scared. I still don't know what that guy was doing there now. I told people about what happened there, but nobody believes me.

The following message was posted by someone claiming to be a police officer in Aomori:

Sugisawa Village exists. It's close to Aomori Airport…

But you must never go looking for it, and please don't enter it half-cocked.

Because if you do, you'll never come back…

MEDIA

There have been several documentaries and even a movie made about Sugisawa Village over the years. It's featured in several manga, multiple TV shows, and you can even play a game on your mobile phone where you try to escape from the village.

You can find a full list of all these at the Japanese Wikipedia site.

WANT EVEN MORE?

Also available in the *Kowabana: 'True' Japanese scary stories from around the internet series*:

Volume One
Volume Two
Volume Three
Origins

Toshiden: Exploring Japanese Urban Legends

The Torihada Files:
Kage

Read new stories each week at Kowabana.net, or get them delivered straight to your ear-buds with the *Kowabana* podcast!

ABOUT THE AUTHOR

Tara A. Devlin studied Japanese at the University of Queensland before moving to Japan in 2005. She lived in Matsue, the birthplace of Japanese ghost stories, for 10 years, where her love for Japanese horror really grew. And with Izumo, the birthplace of Japanese mythology, just a stone's throw away, she was never too far from the mysterious.